"Can I get you anything?"

Yeah, yourself, Drew mentally said.

"I was going to put on a pot of coffee. It looks to be a very late night," Kate added.

It could be, he thought. "Coffee's fine. I'm easy to please."

"Are you really?" she queried with an arched brow. "Somehow I'd imagined you'd be more demanding."

"Oh," he answered, his tone smooth as bourbon, "I can be that, as well. Depends on what's being offered."

"Coffee."

Are you sure? he wondered. "Then coffee it is," he said. *At least for the moment.*

"Make yourself comfortable and I'll be back in a minute."

"I'll be waiting...."

Dear Reader,

What better way to enjoy the last lingering days of summer than to revel in romance? And Special Edition's lineup for August will surely turn your thoughts to love!

This month's THAT'S MY BABY! title will tug your heartstrings. Brought to you by Ginna Gray, *Alissa's Miracle* is about a woman who marries the man of her dreams—even though he doesn't want children. But when she unexpectedly becomes pregnant, their love is put to the ultimate test.

Sometimes love comes when we least expect it—and that's what's in store for the heroines of the next three books. *Mother Nature's Hidden Agenda* by award-winning author Kate Freiman is about a self-assured woman who thinks she has everything…until a sexy horse breeder and his precocious daughter enter the picture! Another heroine rediscovers love the second time around in Gail Link's *Lone Star Lover*. And don't miss *Seven Reasons Why*, Neesa Hart's modern-day fairy tale about a brood of rascals who help their foster mom find happily-ever-after in the arms of a mysterious stranger!

Reader favorite Susan Mallery launches TRIPLE TROUBLE, her miniseries about identical triplets destined for love. In *The Girl of His Dreams*, the heroine will go to unbelievable lengths to avoid her feelings for her very best friend. The second and third titles of the series will be coming your way in September and October.

Finally, we're thrilled to bring you book two in our FROM BUD TO BLOSSOM theme series. Gina Wilkins returns with *It Could Happen To You*, a captivating tale about an overly cautious heroine who learns to take the greatest risk of all—love.

I hope you enjoy each and every story to come!

Sincerely,

Tara Gavin,
Senior Editor

Please address questions and book requests to:
Silhouette Reader Service
U.S.: 3010 Walden Ave., P.O. Box 1325, Buffalo, NY 14269
Canadian: P.O. Box 609, Fort Erie, Ont. L2A 5X3

GAIL LINK
LONE STAR LOVER

SPECIAL EDITION®

Published by Silhouette Books
America's Publisher of Contemporary Romance

To Paula Parasink—who got me into reading category
romances in the first place. Thanks for always being
such a great friend!

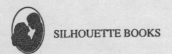 SILHOUETTE BOOKS

ISBN 0-373-24121-6

LONE STAR LOVER

Copyright © 1997 by Gail Link

This edition published by arrangement with Harlequin Books S.A.

® and TM are trademarks of Harlequin Books S.A., used under license.
Trademarks indicated with ® are registered in the United States Patent
and Trademark Office, the Canadian Trade Marks Office and in other
countries.

Printed in U.S.A.

Books by Gail Link

Silhouette Special Edition

Marriage To Be? #1035
Lone Star Lover #1121

GAIL LINK

A bookseller since 1977, Gail realized her dream of becoming a published author with the release of her first book, a historical novel, in 1989.

Gail is a member of the national Romance Writers of America and Novelists, Inc. She has been a featured speaker at many writers' conferences, and several publications have featured her comments on the romance genre, including *Publishers Weekly* and the RWA Report. In 1993 Gail was nominated for the *Romantic Times* Reviewer's Choice Award for Best Sensual Historical.

In addition to being a voracious reader, Gail is also an avid musical theater and movie fan. She would love to hear from her readers, and you may write to her at P.O. Box 717, Concordville, PA 19331.

Prologue

She couldn't get him out of her mind. Like a brand, his image was seared into her brain. There was no escaping the truth—she was his and would be so forever.

Kate Reeves typed the words into her computer, ending the chapter of the latest historical romance that she was working on.

Drained from writing about her fictional heroine's emotional crisis, Kate pushed back her chair and rose from her desk, exhausted. She desperately needed to take a break from the fantasy she'd created.

Besides, Kate thought, glancing at her wristwatch, it was after 4:30 p.m. She'd been at the laptop writing for almost the entire day. It was time to unwind for a while, and maybe grab a salad to ease the rumbling in her stomach. She was meeting her sister-in-law Mariah in Philly for a late dinner, but that wouldn't be for several more hours.

Although Kate usually liked to keep at her computer when her work was cooking, she knew from past experience that after writing an especially tough scene, it was better to walk away, take a breather. Kate had discovered that that was particularly true with this book because she could readily empathize with her heroine's dilemma. Some men *were* unforgettable, no matter how hard one tried to put them aside. They were there, a part of life, like the sun that rose every day. A constant one accepted because there was no other choice.

After shutting off the laptop and her boom box, Kate moved from her spacious office upstairs to the kitchen downstairs. As soon as she did, she was greeted affectionately by her two dogs, both collies, one golden, the other a tricolor mix of black, brown and white.

Kate hunkered down and hugged the animals, rubbing their thick, soft fur. They in turn barked greetings to her, licking her hands and face, wanting to play.

"Guess I've been neglecting you guys today," she said as she stood and grabbed an oversize burgundy sweater from the wooden coatrack that hung on the wall by the kitchen door. "Okay," she said with a smile, "let's go for a walk, then."

The dogs yelped in approval as Kate unlocked the door and stepped outside onto the gravel driveway that led to the two-car garage at the back of her house. The air was chilly, so she pulled a pair of old knit gloves from the pockets of the sweater and slipped them on. Fall had finally arrived here in Chester County. Leaves were already turning; the days were getting shorter.

Kate didn't mind. Autumn was by far her favorite season. She loved the change in the weather, loved the differences in the colors of the trees.

It had been Jack's favorite season, as well.

Some days it was still so hard to believe that he was gone, and had been for almost three years. Kate hugged the sweet memory of her late husband to her heart even as another masculine face gradually replaced Jack's in her mind's eye.

She heard the excited barking of the two dogs as they playfully chased a couple of squirrels around several of the trees that dotted the rolling hills of her property. It wasn't unusual for Kate to see deer grazing along the wooden fence that bordered her land.

Kate glanced up and noticed the wonderful shadings of the sky above. Sunset wouldn't be long in coming. Colors swirled and mixed in a deep palette of rich shades. She loved this part of the day; it always gave her a sense of wonder, of being part of something grander.

She sat down on the cherry parson's bench under a tall, spreading silver maple, crossing one jeans-clad leg over the other, deep in thought.

She'd met *him* at sunset.

Damn! Why couldn't she leave him in the past where he belonged?

"Iceman. Maverick." Kate called the dogs and they came running toward her, bounding quickly over the grass to her side. "Time to go back inside, fellas."

Kate and the dogs walked back up the drive and into the kitchen of her large farmhouse, where she fixed them each a bowl of food and set the dishes on the floor in front of the brick fireplace. The old-fashioned touch of a hearth in the large room added the right blend of warmth and charm.

Kate put a copper kettle on the stove for hot water. She felt like indulging in a big mug of hot chocolate.

While she was waiting for the water to boil, Kate's thoughts drifted back to the characters from her book, recalling the work that she'd done that day.

She'd created, once again, a hero to die for.

At least that's what the heroine of her romance novel thought. He was a man who'd recklessly stolen her heroine's heart the moment he'd claimed her body. A man whom the heroine believed she couldn't have—yet, he was the man she couldn't forget, either. They'd shared one night of dark, dangerous passion that had altered the course of the heroine's life.

Kate breathed a small sigh. That fact hit way too close to home.

Kate hadn't meant to change the description of her fictional hero when she began writing this book. When she'd first conceived the story, her main male character had been tall, just not *so* tall. He'd had straight auburn hair, not the wavy, almost black shade he had now. He'd had blue eyes—not the deep brown of roasted coffee that she now wrote about. Kate had completely altered the physical structure of the man because the image that had crept into her mind was too strong to ignore, and when she wrote, she went with her gut feelings. That was one of the secrets of her success with readers.

Kate hadn't forgotten anything about *him*, and so every detail that had been stored in her brain was unlocked and transferred to the computer, and became the inspiration for her work, whether she wanted it to or not.

She couldn't help herself.

Like a dam that had sprung a leak, sweet, passion-filled memories came flooding back as she wrote, replaying through every gesture, every word she typed.

One good thing, since the book she was writing was set in Colonial Virginia during the Revolutionary War, the hero wasn't going to be a larger-than-life Texan, as in reality *he* was. That would have been entirely too close for comfort.

The kettle whistled, forcing Kate from her reverie. As she poured the boiling water into the mug, she added several spoonfuls of cocoa, stirring the mixture. A handful of tiny marshmallows came next, bobbing in the hot liquid before they slowly melted.

Moments later, Kate sat down at the rectangular oak table with her drink and a small bowl of tossed salad.

It was no use.

Try as she might, Kate couldn't stop thinking about *him*, couldn't help recalling the night they'd first met several months ago, a night forever stamped in her mind.

Chapter One

Kate Reeves hadn't been looking for a lover when she came to Texas.

She was in the middle of a six-state book tour, promoting the release of her first hardcover, which was already climbing the major national bestseller lists when she arrived for a long weekend stop in San Antonio. Wanting to combine business and pleasure, Kate had asked her publisher's publicity manager to extend her time in the city so that she could rest, do some research and have a chance to visit with her good friend, artist Emma Cantrell. Having missed attending Emma's wedding to Texas rancher Burke Buchanan because she'd been on a research trip in England, Kate wanted time to spend with the newlyweds.

They'd met her at the airport; Emma greeted her warmly, happily introducing Kate to her new husband.

It took only one look at her friend's expressive face

to see the whole wonderful love story. Emma was radiant, expecting her first child and madly in love with her handsome husband, who, as Kate could plainly see, was equally in love with his beautiful wife. As Emma had described him, Burke Buchanan was the embodiment of her artistic dreams. Tall, lean, with seductive brown eyes and a sexy voice, he appeared the quintessential Western man.

When Burke left the two women alone to get his car from the airport parking lot, Kate had whispered in a teasing rhetorical tone, since she already knew the answer, "Any more like him at home?"

Emma gave her friend a saucy grin. "I've got the one and only," she answered, "but if you don't mind settling for second best, then yes, I think we could scrape up a few worthy Texans for your consideration. And," she stated in a sly tone, "Burke does have two older brothers, you know."

"Speaking of which," Kate said, glad to be doing so without Burke around since the question involved one of his brothers, "how is Clay taking this marriage?"

Emma folded her slender hands over the mound of her stomach. "He's been incredibly polite and decent about it," she responded, alluding to the fact that before she had met Burke, she'd seriously dated Clay Buchanan. "In fact," Emma confided, "he's even agreed to be one of our child's godfathers. That meant a lot to both of us." Emma paused for a moment, gathering her thoughts. "Burke and Clay finally had a long talk and resolved their estrangement, which was good news to the family. It's been tough on both of them, not to mention their parents and Drew, because the Buchanans are such a close-knit family to begin with."

"I can imagine that it's been tough on you, as well," Kate said sympathetically.

Emma sighed. "It was. I'm very fond of Clay, as you know. But it's all behind us now, thank God."

"I'm so happy that you found what you've been searching for," Kate said.

"So am I," Emma responded. "I love Burke more than I ever thought possible." She spread her fingers over her tummy. "More so each day."

"Don't ever take it for granted," Kate warned in a sober voice, speaking from her own experience, "because you never know how long you have."

When she saw the sad expression on her friend's face, Kate hastily apologized. "Oh, God, Emma, here I am being a real downer when I should be congratulating you on the baby and on your happiness. I'm sorry."

Emma took Kate's hand, squeezing it lightly. "Don't apologize, Kate. I know where you're coming from. Jack's death was hard on you. It's never easy to lose someone you loved as much as you loved him. God knows how I would cope if anything were to happen to Burke."

Emma took a deep breath, plunging ahead with her question. "Have you started seeing anyone else?"

"You're beginning to sound like everyone at home," Kate replied, tilting her head so that she looked away from Emma's keen eyes. "Even my sister-in-law, Mariah, has been after me to go out again." She paused for a moment before continuing, "I can't, Emma. It's still too soon."

"Three years is a long time, Kate."

"Not for me it isn't."

"You haven't met the right man yet."

"I *had* the right man, Emma," Kate responded. "I'm not interested in another."

"Never say never," Emma insisted. "I learned my lesson regarding obstinacy. Love can come when you least expect it."

"You hold that thought," Kate said.

"At least keep an open mind," Emma suggested. "It's gonna be my pleasure to introduce you to Drew tomorrow."

Kate arched one slim brow. "You've invited your brother-in-law to meet me?"

Emma shrugged. "Why not? I think you two will get along famously. You're both writers."

"I'm not interested."

"Tell me that after you've met him," Emma said. "Besides, it's only for dinner."

Kate tilted down her sunglasses and shot Emma an arched look. She just couldn't be mad at her friend. She knew Emma cared about her and wanted to see her happy. Brimming over with her own personal joy, Emma naturally wanted others to be as content as she was. For Kate, it was just that she'd had the love of her life and wasn't looking for another. Frankly, she didn't know if she could ever handle the pain of loving again. Loving left you vulnerable, open to hurt. It also left a considerable void in your soul when it was untimely snatched from you.

For Kate, love was confined to the pages of the romance novels she wrote. It was safer, cleaner, neater that way. While writing, she was in charge and fate responded to her whims. Her readers were guaranteed a happy ending. Kate was all too aware that real life never presented that same guarantee.

"Here comes Burke," Emma said. "Thank God. It's

so damned hot today that I can't wait to get back into that air-conditioned car.'' Emma got to her feet slowly. ''Just wait till you see the Buchanan house. It's really fabulous.'' She hugged Kate again. ''I'm so glad you changed your mind and decided to stay with us rather than take a hotel room.''

''Are you sure that it isn't too much trouble?''

''Nonsense,'' Emma insisted. ''It's a big house. And I've put you in the guest cottage in back, so you can have your privacy. Then, after you've had a chance to rest, we'll drive you to your signing.''

Kate protested softly, ''You don't have to do this, Em.''

''Of course I don't,'' Emma answered her friend with a smile. ''I want to do this for you. Come on. Texans love driving, and it's no big deal to take you to Rolling Oaks Mall.''

''You're sure?''

''Get real, Kate. Of course I'm sure. Who knows when you'll be back here again, so let's enjoy it while we can. Besides,'' Emma admitted, ''it'll be good to have a friend around. We'll be able to spend some time together since Burke won't be staying the entire weekend, anyway.''

''He won't? How come?''

''Jessie, my step-daughter, is riding in her first show this weekend in Austin, and he can't miss that,'' Emma explained. ''We're both so proud of her.''

''And you're not going?''

''No. Jessie understands.''

''Are you sure?'' Kate didn't want to be the cause of any discord in the new family unit.

''I told her that a dear friend was coming to town,

and I asked her if she would be okay with me spending time with you.''

''And she was?''

Emma smiled proudly. ''Right as rain. When she heard that it was you, her grandmother's favorite writer, well, she was upset that she couldn't meet you herself. She declared you 'cool.'''

''Cool?''

''Exactly.''

Kate laughed softly just as Burke pulled up, grabbed her suitcase and tossed it into the back of the Jeep Wagonner. ''Still, it must bother you to miss it.''

Burke helped his wife into the car. Kate smiled at his thoughtfulness and care of Emma as she got into the back seat. That he adored her friend was evident in every gesture, every look he bestowed on Emma. Their closeness brought a tug of sadness to Kate's heart for her own loss even as she reveled in her friend's obvious good fortune.

''Miss what?'' Burke asked as he pulled the car into the lane of traffic exiting the airport.

''I was just explaining to Kate that you wouldn't be able to spend the weekend here due to Jessie's show.''

''Your daughter comes first. I can easily understand that,'' Kate acknowledged.

''Thanks,'' Burke responded in his deep Texas drawl. ''Jessie is really looking forward to this event. It's all she's talked about for the last week.''

Emma looked over her shoulder. ''It'll give us a chance to catch up and play tourists to our hearts' content.''

''The Alamo?'' Kate asked, eager to see the monument she considered Texas's heart and soul.

Emma nodded. ''No trip to San Antone would be

complete without it. And," she added, "I think you'll like the Institute of Texan Cultures, too." Emma faced front again, reaching out her hand and placing it upon her husband's solid jeans-clad thigh. "Tonight we're taking you to dinner along the River Walk to one of our favorite little restaurants. I just know you'll love it, Kate."

"I'm looking forward to it," she responded enthusiastically.

Kate sipped her second margarita as she watched one of the boats as it ferried tourists around the tree-lined river. She heard the excited laughter of children, gradually overshadowed by the music of a strolling mariachi band. A sidewalk art-and-craft show was also taking place on the other side of the river, with stalls overflowing with merchandise. A small bag of one-of-a-kind ornaments from one of the vendors rested under Kate's seat, items she'd purchased for her own Christmas tree this year.

"What a great idea to have dinner outside," Kate remarked, finishing the last of her sizzling chicken fajitas and refried beans.

Emma, drinking a large glass of iced tea, nodded. "It's fun to sit here and people watch. At Christmastime," she said, "the trees along the river are strung with lights. It's all so beautiful." She shot a sideways glance at her husband. "San Antonio in December holds special memories for us."

Burke reached over and took Emma's hand in his, intertwining their fingers. He lowered his voice and whispered something into Emma's ear, bringing a blush to her cheeks.

Kate glanced away, hating to intrude on what was

obviously a private moment between the couple. Doing so, she removed her sunglasses and focused her attention on the sun as it began to set over the river. The sky was streaked with a riot of colors. Just then, the color-dappled sky as a stunning backdrop, a very tall man threaded his way through the outdoor restaurant, coming toward their table.

She knew she was staring at him, but Kate couldn't help herself. He looked like a model, or perhaps an actor with his smooth, dark good looks. He wore a black T-shirt that hugged his wide chest, outlining lean, masculine muscles, jeans that molded the long length of his legs, and black boots, along with a high-watt smile that could light up the approaching darkness single-handedly.

He could just as easily have emerged from the pages of one of the many books she'd written.

Her pulse leapt. He was definitely getting closer.

"Drew—what a surprise!" Emma exclaimed as the man stopped at their table.

So, Kate discovered, momentarily stunned by her instant response to him, this sexy hunk was one of Burke's older brothers. He was devastatingly handsome. He was a man women noticed, evident by the number of female diners who gave him a long, lingering look when he passed their way.

He shook hands with Burke and leaned down to kiss his sister-in-law on the cheek. "I got in earlier than expected, sweetheart, and when I stopped at the house, I was told that you all had gone out to dinner along the Paseo del Rio. I got your message that Burke would be leaving tomorrow, so I thought rather than crash, if I wanted to see you both, I'd better haul a—" he paused, slicing a glance in Kate's direction "—butt and get here tonight."

"I'm glad you did," Emma said approvingly, "especially so that I can introduce you to one of my best friends, Kate Reeves."

Drew came around the small table; he moved closer to Kate and put out his hand. "Glad to meet you, Kate," he said in a voice as deep as he was tall.

Kate craned her neck back to look into his face. He had to be, she guessed, about six foot three. Drew Buchanan was a big man. No doubt about that. Broad shoulders, long legs, a full head of thick, wavy brown hair that was one shade away from being black. He had a strong nose, a wide mouth, deep crinkles in his face when he smiled, and something he shared with his younger brother—a pair of intense brown eyes set beneath wide dark brows.

Drew held her hand for almost a full minute before he released it and sat down next to her, his thigh brushing against hers, setting off a tingle of electricity, as had his hand when it had held hers. It was already a warm and muggy mid-June day, and his presence made it seem even more so to Kate. He looked so cool, and she felt more and more like a limp dishrag.

Their waitress came by to take his order of a cold beer and a thick steak, medium.

"Emma told me that you're a writer," Kate stated by way of an opening conversational gambit.

His cold beer was delivered, and Drew took the opportunity to take a hearty swallow of it before he answered Kate's question. "That's right," he said, looking deeply into her eyes, "I work for *Lone Star Monthly*."

"Doing what?"

"Pretty much whatever I feel like," he responded, his dark eyes focused on her. "Profiles, mostly. Politics. Sports. Entertainment. The usual."

Burke snorted. "Drew's being too modest," he said. "In addition to that he's been in quite a few of the major danger zones of the world. Bosnia. The Middle East. The Gulf War." Burke smiled. "Not to mention that his writing has won numerous awards."

Drew threw his brother a fond glance and shrugged his broad shoulders.

Kate heard the pride in the younger man's voice. She also heard *danger zones*. Was Drew Buchanan a danger junkie? Did he think he was impervious to the violence that all too often erupted from nowhere and claimed lives?

Emma chimed in, "So has Kate."

Drew returned his glance to Kate again. "Do you write?"

"Yes," she answered, allowing her own love of what she did to shine through. "Historical romances under my maiden name, Kathryn Reeves."

"Oh," Drew said, "you're the one that Emma does the covers for?"

"That's me," Kate replied, taking another sip of her margarita.

"You're one of my mother's favorites," Drew stated.

"So Emma tells me."

"What brings you to Texas?" Drew asked as he reached over and picked up one of the remaining corn chips from the almost empty bowl and dunked it into a dish of spicy salsa.

"I'm doing a book tour for my latest, and I'm getting in some research for other books, as well."

"Kate sold over fifty books today at Rolling Oaks Mall," Emma put in.

"That's great," Drew declared, hoisting his beer bottle in salute. "Your husband must be very proud of your success."

"He was," Kate said, her words bittersweet. "I'm a widow, Mr. Buchanan."

"Sorry," he murmured, sounding sincere.

"Thank you," Kate responded politely.

"Signings can be tough. I've interviewed several very successful writers and they all have horror stories to tell about autographings that went south."

"I know what you mean," Kate said. "I'm always happy if I sell at least two copies of a book, because I can remember the days when that would have been quite a lot." At the disbelieving looks thrown her way, Kate protested, "I'm not kidding, really. I've done some signings when all I did was give directions to the nearest bathroom, or tell a customer where to find a certain author."

Sympathetic laughter erupted around the table as the waitress returned with Drew's steak.

As he cut into the meat, he asked, "How long are you here for?"

"Until Monday morning," Kate replied. "Then it's on to Dallas and Forth Worth, Oklahoma City and Tulsa, then New Mexico and finally home."

"Been grueling?" he inquired, easily falling into his journalist mode.

"A bit," Kate admitted. "But it's always fun meeting my readers and seeing some of the cities when I have the chance."

"And it's an excuse for shopping," Emma said with a laugh.

"Thank heavens for plastic," Kate replied.

Emma nodded and yawned.

"I think maybe we'd better call it a night," Burke suggested.

"No, not on my account," Emma protested.

"Darlin'," Burke said in a soothing tone, "you know what the doctor told us. You need your rest." He placed one of his hands on her stomach. "I think he's gonna be a bronc rider when he gets out."

Kate asked, "May I?"

Emma nodded, and Kate put her hand where Burke's had been, feeling the force of the child's kick. She and Jack, she recalled, had talked about having children later in their marriage.

Kate raised her head and looked at Emma's glowing face. She also read the signs of tiredness there.

"That's okay," Kate said. "I'm feeling kind of worn out myself. It's been a long day already."

"Where are you staying?" Drew asked.

"With us," Emma stated.

"Look, I can drop her off at home if you two want to go now," Drew offered. He sliced Kate a glance. "That is, if you'd like to linger here awhile longer?"

"I wouldn't want to put you out," Kate insisted.

"No trouble," Drew responded. "Just let me finish my dinner and I'll be more than happy to take you."

A frisson of unexpected sexual excitement feathered through Kate's veins with his last two words. It was a perfectly acceptable statement, but, for some reason, Drew's deep voice underscored the words with a much different meaning for her.

Burke glanced in Drew's direction. "If you're sure you don't mind?"

Drew replied, "I don't, so let's leave it at that."

"Then," Emma said, reaching over and kissing Kate, "how about we meet for breakfast tomorrow morning?"

Kate nodded. "Sounds good to me."

"What time's good for you?" Emma inquired, standing with Burke's help.

"How about eight-thirty?"

Burke and Emma exchanged glances. "Fine," Emma responded.

Burke shot his brother a sharp look. "See you later, then, Drew?"

"I'll be there in a bit, little brother," Drew answered with an engaging grin.

"They're so great together," Kate said as the other couple walked away, hand in hand.

"That they are," Drew agreed, cutting the remaining part of his steak into two smaller pieces. "Emma's the best thing to happen to my brother since Jessie was born."

"I'm glad to hear you say that."

"It's true," Drew stated, washing down the last bit of beef with what remained in the long-necked beer bottle.

Kate felt slightly awkward, as if she were on a blind date, waiting for him to make the next move.

This was ridiculous, she told herself. She'd been a married woman. It was no doubt the potent sensuality emanating from the man sitting next to her that was causing this reaction. Money, looks, good breeding, intelligence, it all came together in one powerful package that made her aware of Drew as a man. Aware in ways that she hadn't felt in a long time.

It was instant attraction on her part. A jolt of pure sexual desire, Kate rationalized. Hot, raw lust. That had to be the answer. After all, it had been so long since she'd been held by a man, kissed by a man, loved by a man. That was the real reason that she was experiencing this powerful reaction to him.

Kate felt guilty. As if by acknowledging that she was feeling this way she was being somehow unfaithful to Jack's memory.

"Would you like something else?"

Kate hadn't even seen the waitress come back, she'd been so lost in thought. "Nothing for me," she said.

"Just the check," Drew responded.

"The other Mr. Buchanan took care of it," the woman informed them.

"Then, if you're ready?" Drew asked Kate. Rising, he withdrew a bill from his wallet and handed it to the waitress.

"There's no need, sir," she explained, "your brother's already added my tip."

"Keep it," Drew insisted.

"Thank you," she gushed in surprise, tucking the bill into the pocket of her apron.

"That was very generous of you," Kate stated. She knew that he could afford to tip well. Emma had told her about the family that she had married into: the Buchanans were one of Texas's first families—wealthy, prestigious and influential in all arenas.

"I appreciate good service, and," he added, "when I was at grad school I waited tables for almost a month for an article I was writing."

"A Buchanan waiting tables?" Kate asked, curious.

"Being a Buchanan didn't matter too much in New York City."

"You went to school back east?" Somehow Kate would have pegged him as having a down-home, Texas born-and-bred education.

"American studies at Georgetown, and then journalism at Columbia."

Intriguing, she thought. Not simply another pretty face.

"And you?"

"University of Pennsylvania," she replied. "History, with a minor in English literature."

Drew nodded his head, as if approving her choices. "My car's not far from here."

Kate said, "I can get a cab, you know, if you have somewhere else you'd like to go."

Drew looked down at Kate from his imposing height as she rose from her chair. "I promised that I'd see you back, Kate," Drew responded. "A Texan, especially a Buchanan," he emphasized, "always keeps his word."

As they walked along the river, Kate couldn't help but notice the number of couples strolling arm in arm, with eyes only for each other. Young, old and in-between, everyone seemed to be paired off.

She glanced down at the band of gold that circled her third finger on her left hand. She'd been part of a pair once. A good pair. Her marriage had been happy, fulfilling.

"This way," Drew said as he gently touched her shoulder, leading her toward a nearby parking lot.

Kate's eyes opened wider as she quickly glanced at his car. It was a vintage Jaguar, black and sleek.

He noticed her staring admiringly at his vehicle. "Like it?"

"I've always wanted to ride in one like this," she confessed.

"Get in, then," he said as he unlocked the door.

Kate slid into the butter-soft leather seat and fastened the seat belt. Drew slid in beside her, starting the engine, which purred to life. She had a fondness for Jags, and a secret wish to own one. Jack had teased her about it, laughing with her about "someday."

The drive to the Buchanan house on King William Street was far too short. It would have been fun to see what this machine could do on an open road.

Drew pulled up in front of the entrance and turned into the tree-lined drive, and as Kate started to say, "Thank you," he interrupted her.

"I'll see you inside."

Before she could protest, Drew was out of the driver's side.

Kate got out as Drew held the door open, giving her a hand from the low-slung car.

As they made their way across the walkway that led to the cottage, Kate sighed. The warm night air was softened by the smell of the fragrant flowers that dominated the garden.

Kate stood in the doorway of the small, two-storey guest cottage after she'd unlocked the front door, then half turned toward Drew. An outside light burned softly in an iron sconce. "It was nice meeting you," she murmured politely, holding out her hand.

Drew took it, then did something completely unexpected. He bent down and kissed her softly on the mouth. It was a quick brush of his lips over hers, over almost as soon as it began.

"Great meeting you, too, Kate," he said with that engaging half grin, releasing her hand. "Good night." He turned and walked back down the pathway, out of her life.

Kate walked in and shut the door quickly, her heart pounding.

It was just a friendly kiss. Nothing more. Nothing less. No big deal in the scheme of things.

If that was so, then why was she trembling?

Chapter Two

Drew slipped out of his bed, unable to fall asleep.

The reason was simple—he couldn't stop thinking about the woman in the guest house. Every time he'd tried to close his eyes, he saw her face.

And what a face it was. Intriguing. Captivating. There was a lot going on behind those deep blue eyes of hers, depths to be explored, secrets to be shared.

What about her mouth? Kissable. Incredibly so. And soft. So soft.

He stood in front of the window that overlooked the garden, and beyond that, the cottage. Drew turned his head, staring back at the deep green sheets that covered his bed. He could almost see her thick mane of curly golden blond hair spread over his pillow. He could almost see her tall, lithe form lying there, the sheet exposing one soft white shoulder to his gaze.

Get a grip, Buchanan, Drew chided himself, his eyes

back on the upper floor of the guest cottage, where lights shone from one of the bedrooms. It was the one closest to the outside stairs. The big room. Obviously, she wasn't sleeping yet, either.

She had to have felt the same intense reaction he'd had, he reckoned. How could she not have? It was hot. Strong. Demanding. The kind of instant electricity that signals potentially great sex. The atavistic connection of male to female.

There was no doubt in his mind. He wanted her. Then and there. Hot and fast, at first. Later, long and slow, lingering over the finer points of their erotic dance.

He wondered what she was wearing for bed. Satin? Lace? Nothing? Tonight, she'd been casually dressed: a white T-shirt tucked into a crisp olive-green cotton twill skirt. A pair of casual sandals, revealing toes painted the same shade of ripe red as her mouth.

Drew took a deep breath, exhaling slowly, his fantasies unwinding with a delicious abandon until the light went out in the cottage.

He moved away from the window, wondering if he should try to go back to bed. He shook his head, deciding against that idea. What he could really use was a drink of something cold. Iced tea. The housekeeper always had a pitcher or two in the fridge. Maybe that would cool the overworking of his heated imagination.

He grabbed a pair of jeans from the chair and pulled them on over his tapered boxer shorts, then walked barefoot out the door to his bedroom, heading for the backstairs to the kitchen.

When Drew got there, there was already a light on. Moving inside, he saw that another member of his family shared his late-night idea.

"Junior getting hungry?" Drew asked as he withdrew a large glass from the cabinet.

Emma sat at the table, munching on a piece of cold fried chicken and a jalepeño corn-bread muffin with butter. A tall glass of milk was in front of her. "You could say that," she answered with a smile. She patted her stomach with one hand, the gleam of her wedding ring catching in the overhead light. "The little fellow was restless tonight, insisting I feed him. So, if I wanted some peace eventually, I thought it best to give in to his demands."

"So sure it's a boy?"

Emma tilted her head, giving Drew a considering glance as she watched him fill his glass with iced tea. "Hints have been dropped, shall we say, that it had better be."

"From Burke?"

Emma smiled at her husband's name. "No. He only wants this baby to be healthy, though I have a sneaking suspicion that he would like a boy this time. Your niece, Jessie, insists that it be a boy. She wants a brother, which she's told me repeatedly. Noah and Santina have hinted that they'd like a grandson, as well."

"Don't you want to know for sure?" Drew swallowed the tea, finishing half the glass by the time he was done. "I couldn't stand not knowing as soon as possible."

"Funny, Kate said the same thing to me earlier." Emma watched Drew's face as she spoke her friend's name. When she saw the sudden flare of awareness in his eyes, she deepened her smile. Her brother-in-law was quite a catch. Sexy. Sophisticated. Sharp as a proverbial tack. Just the type of man who might help get Kate back into life. "You two have something in common."

"Impatience?" he said with a laugh, "or curiosity?

What do you think?'' He leaned back against the counter, one bare foot crossed over the other.

"Probably both, I'd be willing to bet," Emma observed.

"And you'd more than likely be right," he admitted. His sister-in-law was keenly observant. Stemmed from her being a painter, he assumed.

"Look, we haven't had a chance to talk for a while," she said, nibbling on the chicken, "so why don't you join me?" She took a sip of the milk, her blue-green eyes fixed on him. "How's San Antonio's number-one bachelor? Are you currently seeing anyone special?"

Drew shook his head as he refilled his glass, grabbing a corn-bread muffin for himself and taking a seat opposite her.

"Too bad," she murmured sympathetically, inwardly glad of the news.

"Why?" He took a generous bite of the muffin. "Just because you and baby brother are happy in the married state is no reason to think that's what I'm looking for."

Emma sliced him a direct glance. "What are you looking for, then?"

"No complications," Drew answered with a grin. "I like my life just the way it is."

"Footloose and fancy free?"

"You got it. I like being able to pick up and go where I please, when I please. No strings."

"Don't you ever get lonely?"

Drew chuckled. "I'm a big boy, Emma. Trust me, I know how to find a lady when I want one."

"I don't imagine you have trouble in that department."

He smiled. "Never had before. I like women. They like me. It's very simple."

Emma grinned. "The bigger they are, the harder they fall."

"Bull."

"Someday..."

"But no time soon, believe me," he assured her.

Emma had seen the sexual sparks fly between Kate and Drew when she introduced them. Maybe, my dear brother-in-law, it'll be sooner than you think, she mentally added.

She uttered her next question as delicately as she could, afraid that she might be crossing some kind of line. "You're careful, aren't you, Drew?"

He didn't take offense. "Very. I take precautions."

Emma heaved a small sigh of relief. "Good."

Shifting topics, Drew asked, "So, how long have you known her?"

"Kate?"

"Yes."

"About five years or so, I suppose."

Drew tried to maintain a casual tone. "How long's she been a widow?"

"Three years now."

"How'd it happen?"

Good, Emma thought, Drew was intrigued. "He was a Philadelphia cop who was killed in the line of duty."

She'd been a cop's wife. Drew had interviewed several before for a piece he'd written a couple of years ago. It took guts to be married to a man in that line of work. Guts and a ton of faith. "God, that must have been tough."

"It was. Kate was devastated when he died. If she hadn't had her work, along with her family and friends, I think she might have died, as well."

"But she didn't."

"No. Kate's a strong person. I just wish..."

"What?" he interjected.

Emma shook her head, rising. "Nothing. Forget it." She yawned, glancing at the clock on the wall. "I'd better be getting back to bed if I want to get up and see Burke off, then be ready for the sightseeing day with Kate." She left her plate in the sink after scraping off the remains of the chicken into the garbage. That done, she leaned over and kissed Drew on his stubble-darkened cheek and squeezed his shoulder. "It's so good seeing you home, safe and sound. After that scare in Bosnia, we weren't sure, you know."

Drew understood what Emma was referring to—while on assignment in that war-torn country, he'd been involved in a minor skirmish. Shots had been fired, and he'd been held hostage for a few hours until the situation was defused without bloodshed. For him, it was all part of the deal when reporting on a story in a country ravaged by violence and strife. Sometimes it was difficult remembering that his family might be worried.

"Actually," he admitted, "it's nice being home for a change."

"Are you staying put for a while?"

"I think so. Depends on how this next story develops." He drained the remaining tea from the glass and rose. "What time's Burke leaving?"

"Around eight, he said."

"Maybe I'll see you then." He'd planned on looking up a few friends tomorrow, see what was happening. Perhaps, he thought, he could postpone that. After all, the ladies might need a skilled guide on their tour of the city. It wouldn't be anywhere neighborly to leave them all alone to fend for themselves. Besides, it was the least he could do for a friend of one of his family.

Drew smiled in anticipation. Could prove to be interesting.

Kate dressed in a pair of white cotton shorts and a teal blue T-shirt with a brown braided belt around her slim waist. A pair of matching teal-colored socks, and white canvas sneakers finished the outfit. Her thick, slightly past shoulder-length hair was caught up in a braided satin ponytail holder.

She was joining Emma for breakfast, so she hurriedly gathered her oversize tan canvas saddlebag purse, checking to make sure she had her camera and notebook inside.

Would he be there?

Kate walked outside to the balcony, stealing a glance in the direction of the back of the main house. She'd seen a light burning in one of the upstairs bedrooms late into the evening last night. Whose room had that been? Drew Buchanan's?

So what if it had been? That was no concern of hers.

Angry at the direction of her thoughts, Kate stepped back inside the room and locked the French doors behind her.

Who was she kidding? She couldn't deny the quiver of sexual sparks that had struck her when she first saw him, when their hands had met. And, later, when he'd kissed her. A hot, swift kiss that had left its mark. Like sun on snow, she'd melted inside. No big deal, really, she told herself. A normal reaction. It had been a long time since a man's lips had touched hers, since a man had looked at her like that.

No, that wasn't true, she admitted. There had been men who'd looked at her as if they'd wanted to get close to her, eventually bed her. Kate couldn't pretend that she wasn't attractive. Her mirror told her otherwise, and to ignore that fact would have been stupid. What had hurt was that some of the men who'd offered to help her *deal* with Jack's passing had been his friends. Strangers, she could have understood, coming on to her. But when his supposed *friends* did, it ripped at her already bruised soul. Some men wanted a woman, and when they did, any woman would do. Sex was a simple enough need. But not for her. Since her husband's death, she'd been frozen inside. She missed her husband. Ached to have his arms around her, his body loving hers.

That wasn't going to happen ever again. She'd faced that bitter fact head-on.

No one had stirred even a modicum of interest within her since Jack's death.

Until last night.

Until a stranger had entered her world and rocked its foundations by his mere existence. Until he'd touched her, kissed her and stirred to life dormant needs.

Drew Buchanan.

There was a man who could melt butter. His wicked grin hinted at a deep knowledge of the female sex; his devil-may-care eyes promised delight; his tall body offered temptation.

Kate understood want; she wrote about it in her books. The unvarnished truth was that she wanted him. Like a light bulb being switched on, she felt the power of his attraction illuminating the dark corners of her feminine core, corners she'd thought were closed off since Jack's passing.

She'd just have to ignore the messages her body was sending to her brain. She wasn't an impetuous teenager, pining for her first crush. Sexual chemistry—that's all it was. Powerful, acute chemistry that had hit her with the force of a well-placed arrow. Square and true.

It would be best to ignore it. That was the wisest and safest course, the one that she would follow. Anything else was out of the question.

She smelled of gardenias. That, he realized, was Kate Reeves's signature scent. Drew inhaled the fragrance as soon as he stepped into the dining room. Strong, but not overpowering. Very, very female.

"Good morning, ladies."

Kate snapped her head up from her plate of *huevos rancheros*. Drew Buchanan was even better-looking than she recalled. In the morning light he was intensely male. Dressed in a black T-shirt and jeans, he could easily be mistaken for a construction worker or a ranch hand. His dark hair was damp, as if he hadn't been long out of the shower. A silver-and-gold Rolex gleamed on his wrist. On his right hand, he wore a large square gold signet ring. She could read the letter *B* engraved in Gothic script.

He had great hands, Kate observed. Big. Capable. Long fingers and wide palms. *All the better to touch you with, my dear.*

Good gracious—where had that thought sprung from? He was hardly the big bad wolf. Or was he?

"Good morning, Drew," Emma returned his greeting.

He joined them at the table, accepting the large mug of coffee from the Buchanan's housekeeper, Selena Sanchez.

"Can I get you anything special, Drew?" Selena asked as she refilled Kate's cup.

Kate smiled at the cozy informality between Selena and Drew. She liked that this family didn't stand on ceremony. It made it easier to adjust to having someone wait on her rather than fixing her own meal.

"Eggs and bacon will do me fine. You do remember how I like them, don't you?" he said in a softly teasing voice as he added a generous amount of cream to his coffee.

Selena's full lips curved into a smile. "As if I could ever forget how you liked anything," she answered.

There was an undercurrent to the conversation that Kate immediately picked up on. It went beyond just friendly—there was a certain dash of intimacy that Kate thought she detected in their tone. Had they had a relationship in the past? Not that it was any business of hers if they had, she acknowledged. Drew was a healthy male; Selena was a very attractive female, albeit a very much married woman. When Emma had made the introductions yesterday, Kate had met Selena's husband, Ramon, the handyman-cum-gardener for the Buchanan's San Antonio house.

"Anything more for you, Miss Reeves?"

Kate shook her head at the friendly inquiry. "No thank you, Selena. I'm fine."

"And you, Miss Emma?"

Emma's mouth kicked up in a small smile. "Maybe just another one of those delicious orange muffins, if you wouldn't mind?"

"Of course not. Coming right up." Selena took a step away from the table and stopped by Drew's seat. "We all lit candles and prayed to the Holy Mother that you would be returned back where you belonged."

Kate's curiosity got the best of her. When Selena left the room, she asked, "What was that about?"

Drew shrugged. "Nothing, really."

Emma threw him an exasperated glance. "Yeah, sure,

Mr. Modesty.'' She quietly explained the incident that the housekeeper was referring to.

Kate listened. On one hand, she was fascinated by the tale; on the other, she was slightly chilled. Here was another man who obviously didn't mind risking life and limb for the job he loved. She knew the type all too well.

"I thought I'd tag along with you ladies today, if you don't mind?" Drew buttered a slice of toast from the silver rack on the table.

Emma raised a reddish-brown brow. "I've got no problems with that. How about you, Kate?"

There was no way Kate could gracefully refuse his offer without seeming inhospitable. She couldn't very well admit to Emma that she had the oh-so-definite hots for her brother-in-law despite her better judgment. That spending more time with him might only reinforce the attraction.

In a neutral tone, she responded, "Okay by me."

"Then, that's settled," Emma stated, a satisfied smile on her face. Her matchmaking plans were working out better than she'd hoped. If they didn't connect, it wouldn't be for want of trying on her part. "We'll leave after everyone's finished breakfast."

Several hours later, a long morning of sightseeing behind them, the trio stopped and had a relaxed lunch at another one of San Antonio's smaller establishments. While they waited for their meals, each ordered a large glass of iced tea.

"I can't believe how much the Alamo affected me," Kate said, adding another slice of lemon to her tea. "I gotta confess that I got goose bumps standing there."

"I felt the same way when I first went there," Drew

admitted, sharing her enthusiasm. "It's as if it's alive with the souls of the men who died there."

"Exactly. Touching the walls was like having a connection to the past. There was an energy, a sort of doorway if you will to their heroic spirits."

"Can I hazard a guess that you'll be using the Alamo in an upcoming book?" Emma ventured.

Kate smiled. "Could be."

"We've got a pretty good collection of books on early Texas history back at the house," Drew stated. "I'm sure my folks wouldn't mind if you wanted to borrow them for research."

Kate's eyes connected with Drew's across the width of the booth. "Thank you."

"My pleasure."

Pleasure. God, Kate wondered, sipping her tea, why did he have to use that word? It conjured up images in her mind of lazy afternoons and ripe kisses. Of hot days and even hotter nights. Of passion reaching ever higher heights. Of storms and squalls, tossing and tumbling all in their wake. Satisfaction so overwhelming one lost touch with reality.

"Kate?"

"I'm sorry," she said, a slight touch of color tinging her cheeks. "I was off somewhere."

"Plotting?" Emma asked, munching on a thin breadstick.

"In a manner of speaking."

"It's the influence of Texas," Emma commented. "I've found myself taking a more historical tone in some of my paintings lately. Living on the ranch has given me a new perspective."

"Not to mention having my brother as a model," Drew added with a grin.

"That, too," Emma agreed. "I don't think I'll ever get tired of painting him."

"Do you use real people in your books, Kate?"

Kate's gaze met Drew's once more. "Sometimes."

"In what way?"

"Any way that serves the story," she responded, opening up. "It could be the tone of a voice." Like yours, she wanted to say. It was sexy and compelling, deep and evocative. The voice of a hero, without doubt. "Or the color of someone's hair." Brown so dark it was like melted chocolate. "And eyes." Alive with the twinkle of a thousand tiny stars. "It could be the build." Kate stared at Drew's wide shoulders and broad chest. "How someone talks." With the hint of a Texas drawl beneath the smooth, polished surface. "Or how they carry their body." With a fluid charm, as if they were comfortable in their own skin.

"Interesting," he murmured.

Her tongue snaked out and wet her lips. "It can be if you choose the right physical model."

"Do you ever find yourself attracted to the man you chose?"

"For the hero, you mean?"

"Yes."

"Of course," she responded honestly. "That's why I use them. It's fun to let one's imagination run wild."

"And safe," he shot back.

"Not always." It wouldn't be safe with you, she thought.

Emma inquired, "Did you ever use Jack?"

Kate gave her friend a bittersweet smile. "Constantly. His beautiful smile. His tender touch. His great laugh."

"Your ideal man?" Drew asked softly. He was suddenly, puzzlingly annoyed that her late husband still held such sway over her.

"He didn't walk on water if that's what you're implying," Kate asserted in a calm, clear voice.

"I didn't mean to suggest..." He started to apologize.

"Here's your pizza, folks." The twenty-something waitress interrupted the conversation as she placed the steaming platter onto the table, along with another pitcher of iced tea. "Enjoy it," she said, and left.

"Cut me a big slice, Drew," Emma ordered softly, anxious to keep things on the right path. "My little cowboy is really starving."

Drew shifted gears, grinning as he complied. "I think you're using him as an excuse to indulge, my dear."

Emma shot him a conspiratorial look. "I know." Taking the piece that he cut, Emma took a bite and then said, "I think that you might like to see the El Mercado next, Kate. It's fun and very close by."

"Real touristy," Drew commented as he took a slice for himself.

"That's okay by me. After all, that's what I am," Kate insisted, "a plain old tourist. Just passing through as they say."

"Hardly plain," Emma interjected, "since not every tourist who comes here has a book on the *New York Times* bestseller list."

"Or hardly old," Drew declared. "You're what? Thirty, tops?"

Kate smiled. "Off by a few years. I'm thirty-three."

Drew lifted a dark brow. "I'm two up on you."

"Soon to be three, right?" Kate asked.

"Next month," Drew confirmed. "July 23."

"Aren't you the twenty-eighth?" Kate asked Emma.

"Yes."

"And what about you, Kate?" Drew chewed his slice of sausage-and-pepperoni pizza, his eyes on the woman sitting opposite him. He watched as her tongue wrapped itself around a dangling string of melted mozzarella. Damn! He couldn't believe he was finding the way she ate pizza erotic.

"October 17. A Libra."

"Balance and beauty," Drew recited. He wondered about the first, knowing she already possessed the second. Was she all cool self-restraint in bed? Or were her scales tipped to favor the hungry, heated power of passion in that arena?

Discovering the answer suddenly became very important to Drew. He picked up another slice of pizza. Very important, indeed.

Chapter Three

The cool water beat down upon Kate's body, adding a measure of relief from the hot, humid day she'd spent traipsing around San Antonio. It had been, conversely, equal parts fun and agony.

The fun part had been spending time with Emma, shopping at the various market stalls at El Mercado, haggling with some of the vendors for merchandise, discussing cover treatments and plot lines as they strolled through the streets of La Villita.

The agony had been in spending so much time with Drew. His presence continually tilted at her windmill of private space. She was so aware of him—of the movement of his body, of the way he smiled, of the way he had of melting her inside with just a word or a look.

Lathering her hair, Kate recalled the wild leap of her pulse when he'd come up behind her as she was investigating a small enameled inkwell at one of the stalls.

His hand had touched hers as she reached for it, electricity shooting through her fingers. She'd almost dropped the object, holding on to it by sheer luck.

"Do you collect them?"

She'd wet her lips, examining the design of the piece. "Uh-huh," she murmured. She'd lifted the lid, pretending that his nearness wasn't sending shivers of awareness through her body.

"Why?" he inquired, his natural questioning nature coming to the fore. "How'd you get started?"

Kate turned her head, tilting it up to look into his face. Again, she was struck by those eyes. Laughing eyes. Even when he was being serious, there would be a hint of exuberance lurking there. He was so alive, she thought. So vital, vigorous and, most especially, virile.

It was that virility that worried her. It tempted, pulling her ever closer, ever nearer to the source.

"My grandmother gave me one, along with my first fountain pen, when my first short story was published in my high school magazine. Gran said it was to remind me that it all started with the written word, the act of communicating with a pen on paper."

"I like that."

"So did I," she admitted, glad, for some unknown reason, that he shared her sentiment.

"So, you've collected them ever since?"

She nodded her head. "Yes."

"Do you want this one?" Drew leaned closer, whispering in her ear.

"I think so."

"I give you a good price, *señorita,*" the merchant stated, eager to make the sale.

Drew had slipped one arm around her shoulders. Even now, in her shower, Kate thought she could still feel the imprint of his hand sliding along the fabric of her T-shirt, the current running through the cotton to her skin below.

He'd spoken to the man in rapid-fire Spanish. Though she didn't understand, Kate had a good idea what was going on. Bargaining. Heads shook. Shoulders shrugged. Eyes narrowed. Eventually, smiles broke out all around.

When Drew quoted her the final price, it was almost half off what was on the tag.

"I'm impressed," she said with wonder in her tone.

"It was nothing," he admitted. "When I was much younger, I watched my mother at flea markets or antique fairs, shopping for items for her interior design business. She was hell-on-wheels with dealers, getting the best bargains for her clients. All you have to know is how to haggle and be willing to engage in it. What really makes it fun is doing it in the sellers' native tongue."

"Speaking of which, was that all you were discussing?" Kate asked. For some reason, she'd had an idea that she was being talked about as well as the merchandise.

Drew laughed. "Señor Sandoval was admiring your beauty in a most complimentary fashion."

"Really?"

"Trust me."

Ah, that was the rub—if only she could. Or it might be more apt to wonder if she could trust herself.

"Let me get it for you," Drew urged, reaching for his wallet. "A souvenir of your trip."

"That's quite all right," Kate had responded, her own wallet at the ready. "I'd rather pay for it myself, if you don't mind."

Drew acquiesced gracefully. "Go for it, then."

She'd bought the item, knowing that whenever she looked at it, it would remind her of that day with him.

Rinsing the shampoo out of her hair, Kate grabbed hold of a towel and wrapped it around her wet locks. She used another fluffy pima towel to dry off her body, letting it fall to the floor while she dusted on body powder, her favorite blend, scented with gardenia. Stroking the puff along her skin, she could almost imagine that it was the touch of a man's fingers skimming along her flesh. Soft and gentle, enticing, pampering.

God, what was going on? she demanded of herself.

She was being just a tad over the top with her fertile imagination.

Hormones. That's all it was. A chemical clicking of pheromones. Basic and elemental.

Kate pulled on a pair of French-cut cotton panties, then added her bra. Tonight it would only be she and Emma for a relaxed dinner. Drew had a previous invitation and had already left the house. She'd watched him from the safety of her window as he fired up his Jag and drove off.

Kate imagined him tearing down the highway, wind blowing his dark hair, a grin on his face as his smooth machine ate up the miles to his destination effortlessly.

And as she rubbed moisturizer into her skin, she knew she wanted to ride again with him. Feel the power of the car and of the man driving it. Let her guard down, her control slip. Roll with the flow, wherever it took her.

Kate bent over and fluffed her hair, rubbing the towel against her scalp, satisfied that she'd gotten out the excess moisture. She straightened, looking at her reflection in the mirror over the pedestal sink.

All a sweet, noncommitted fantasy. She wasn't going anywhere with him. Monday morning she would be getting on a plane to finish her tour. Drew Buchanan would be just a pleasant, somewhat disturbing memory that would fade as time passed.

Still, it was interesting to play "what if?"

"Where are you, Drew?"

He turned his head at the sultry voice. "I'm right here, darlin'," he drawled in response.

"Somehow, sugar, I doubt that." The woman joined him on the wooden balcony that circled one side of the house, overlooking the hills, the bright lights of the city in the distance. "I would ask what's her name, except that I know you'd never waste that much energy on a woman. Not when you've had so many."

"Meow, Melanie."

She jabbed him playfully in the ribs. "It's the truth. Don't I know for certain?" She alluded to the fact that while each might have been tempted, they'd remained friends rather than spoil it with an affair.

Drew turned and glanced down at the petite brunette, a slinky designer dress lovingly caressing her slim body. "Honey, we would have eaten each other alive."

"Probably," Melanie agreed, sipping her champagne, her sharp green eyes filled with sass. "But it would have been fun while it lasted."

He smiled. "We'll never know for sure now, will we?" He was referring to the large diamond on Melanie's ring finger. The party was to celebrate her engagement to a scion of a Texas oil company.

"Oh, well," she said, clinking her fluted glass to his, "that's the breaks, honey." Her tone held traces of her Georgia roots. "Seriously, though, I'm glad you could make it this evening. When you called last night and said you didn't think that you'd be able to come, I was plenty upset.''

He laughed softly. ''I had a change of plans.''

''Oh,'' she asked, her reporter's sense of a story roused, ''was I wrong before? *Is* there a lady involved?''

''Don't you ever get tired of asking questions, Mel?''

''It's my job, sugar,'' she retorted. ''You know that. Besides, isn't that the way you earn your daily bread, too?''

''Touché.''

''So come on, tell me. What's on your mind?''

It wasn't a what, he thought. It was most definitely a *who*. A very sexy who. One who wouldn't stop invading his thoughts, no matter where he was. He'd been planning on blowing off the party last night; then, after spending the afternoon in Kate's company, Drew had decided that he needed a break. A chance to clear his head. Get out and see some friends, especially female friends.

''Drew?'' Melanie stepped closer. ''Is something bothering you? You know that you can talk to me.''

He shrugged his wide shoulders. ''There's nothing to tell.''

''Going all Buchanan on me?''

Drew laughed. ''Now, what the hell is that supposed to mean?''

''Putting up a No Trespassing sign, sugar. I've seen your younger brother Burke do it on occasion. And Clay, too. Whenever you feel someone's getting too close.''

''Bull.''

''Sling it all you want, sugar,'' she countered, ''it's the truth, so help me.''

''Darlin','' a male voice spoke behind them, ''there

is someone I'd like you to meet. You don't mind, do you, Drew?''

Drew shrugged. "Thanks, Bradley, for getting Miss Nosy Buns off my case.''

Melanie arched him a look. "Don't think this lets you off the hook, sugar. I'll be back to you later, I promise. And this time, I want details.''

When she departed, arm-in-arm with her fiancé, Drew took the opportunity to sneak out of the now-noisy space, filling with people. He wandered along the wooden deck, watching a couple stealing a kiss in a corner.

Passion. Calling for the here and now. Unable to resist its driving urge.

That's what he felt, passion rising. An intense urge to be with Kate Reeves. To feel her silken skin, to smell the perfume lingering there. To run his hands through her thick curls, anchoring his hands in the mass of it. To kiss that inviting mouth, send his tongue on a sweet exploration of its depths.

Dammit! Drew could feel the powerful stirring in his body. It didn't matter that she was safely ensconced in his family's guest house, miles away. He could feel her. Here. Within him.

He needed something stronger than champagne, he decided, walking through a set of French doors. A good shot of bourbon might do the trick, wipe away her image, at least temporarily. Melanie usually kept a setup in her entertainment room, he recalled.

Flicking on the light, Drew found the small bar. Pouring himself a large measure of spirit into the squat amber glass, he began to drink it when his eyes fell on a paperback on the nearby side table.

Crossing the few steps, he leaned down and picked

up the volume. It was one of Kate's. Her name was blazoned in gold embossed letters, along with the title: *One Proud Star.* The painting was one of Emma's. He recognized her style, the meticulous detail, the lush sensuality of the couple and their surroundings.

Well, he wondered, what kind of writer was Kate?

All he had to do was open the book to find out.

He took another swallow of the drink, the aged Kentucky bourbon hitting his throat smoothly.

There didn't appear to be a bookmark or pages turned down in the well-read paperback. He supposed Melanie was done with it.

No harm, then, in just taking a look.

Settling down on the love seat, he opened the book, reading the dedication page.

> To Jack: always my knight in shining armor. I love you forever! Thanks for giving me Ireland.

So, this book had been for her husband.

Drew turned the page and read the first few lines.

Within a few minutes, he'd read the entire prologue of the novel, pleasantly surprised at her talent. She was, he judged, a damn good writer. She had him inside her characters' heads, making him feel what was happening in the clash of cultures between the English and Irish in medieval times.

Drew put his drink down, unfinished. He had to read more, but not here where anyone could come in and disturb him. He didn't think Melanie would mind if he borrowed the book. When he was done reading it, he'd give it back.

Spying a notepad next to the portable phone, he hastily jotted Melanie a note, explaining that he'd purloined her copy of the book and promising to return it within a few days.

For research purposes, he'd scribbled.

Drew smiled. Of a sort.

"So, what do you think about Drew?"

Kate studied the tall glass of iced tea she held in her hand. "He seems quite nice."

"Nice? What a really pedestrian word," Emma protested.

"What would you like me to say?"

"How about you think he's one sexy guy."

Kate smiled. "Okay. He is."

Emma groaned. "There. Was that so hard to admit?"

"Not really." Kate sipped at her tea. It was going on nine-thirty; she and Emma had had a quiet dinner here in the garden, surrounded by the profusion of flowers, beneath a spreading live oak. They sat on comfortable chairs, plumped by thick cushions.

"Good. I kinda thought you two might hit it off."

Kate leveled a semiwithering glance at her friend. "Drew Buchanan's a hard man to ignore."

"You're right about that. In fact," Emma mused, "the whole family's kind of hard to ignore. All very distinct personalities." Emma's lips curved into a smile. "All very Texan, from their heads to their boots."

"Confident. Sure of their place in the scheme of things," Kate ventured.

"Exactly."

"No wimps allowed."

Emma laughed. "You got that right." She sipped at her glass of ice-cold milk. "We'll have to get you out to the ranch sometime. There's a treasure trove of material out there to fill several books. Diaries. Letters.

Photographs. Even old newspaper clippings. Tons of stuff. It would make great fodder for novels, believe me. I've used some things as inspirations for paintings.''

Kate mused, ''If you were to paint Drew, how would you see him?''

Emma considered that idea. ''Hmm. That's an intriguing notion. Burke was easy. He's a quintessential Western man. Clay, well, he'd be the captain of a ship, sure and confident as he helms the various Buchanan enterprises. Drew?'' she gave it another moment's conjecture ''—a knight, I think.''

Kate was intrigued by Emma's choice. ''Why that?''

''Because he's always looking for dragons to slay, new challenges to meet, whether he's aware of it or not. Though I haven't known him quite as long, I know Drew isn't afraid to take a stand or make his mark. I admire that.''

''He's lucky to have you in his corner.''

Emma sliced a sideways glance in her friend's direction. ''I'm in your corner, too, Kate.''

''Thanks.''

''No, really. I am.''

''I know,'' Kate stated. ''I appreciate that.''

Emma yawned, her third in as many minutes. ''Sorry to be such a wet blanket, but I think I'll go upstairs and go to bed. All this walking today's worn me out.'' She eased herself out of the chair, one hand on her swollen belly beneath the loose cotton jumper she wore over her camp shirt.

Kate rose also. ''It was fun. Thanks for giving me the tour.''

''Thank Drew. He certainly knows this town like the back of his hand. I've often thought it funny that each brother has marked out his own territory in Texas, if you will. Burke has the Hill Country ranch; Clay loves Houston, and Drew prefers San Antonio.''

''Interesting.''

''Yes,'' Emma replied, ''isn't it? Perhaps we can get Drew to drive you around the countryside tomorrow, show you a little more of the area.''

''That's quite all right,'' Kate protested. ''I'm sure he has better things to do with his time than play tour director. Besides, spending time with you is why I made the long stopover.''

''I want you to get the most out of this trip that you can,'' Emma replied.

''I'm sure I will.''

Emma smiled slyly. ''So am I.''

Kate watched her friend walk away, and then headed back to the guest cottage. She wondered if Emma were deliberately setting her up with Drew. Playing matchmaker.

Once inside the cozy little house, she flicked on the radio, dialing around until she found a station she wanted to listen to. It was still too early for her to go to bed herself, so she decided that she would take this time to write. Her laptop rested on the low coffee table in the living room. Inside, the temperature was cool, thanks to the efficient air-conditioner.

Should she want anything to eat later, the refrigerator was well stocked with a supply of food, and a large pitcher of freshly brewed iced tea, courtesy of Selena.

Kicking off her sandals, Kate settled herself on the floor. She relaxed her back up against the cozy chair behind her.

As she flipped up the screen, she turned the machine on, waiting for the material of her latest historical romance novel to appear. She was almost finished the book, with less than a hundred pages or so to go. The chapter she was working on was an important love scene, with her hero and heroine making love for the first time. She'd set the mood. Now all she had to do was start typing.

He brushed his knuckles against her cheek, skimming them along her soft skin. Tonight she was his. Their long wait was at an end.

He kissed her, gently at first, then with increasing ardor, until he heard her deep sigh of surrender. "Tell me you want this as much as I do," he whispered against her neck, his mouth nibbling her delicate skin.

"Of course I do," she answered her lover-to-be. "More than you can ever know."

He smiled. "That's all I needed to hear."

"What about 'I love you'?" she asked, her eyes lost in his.

"I knew that already, me darlin'," he declared. "You wouldn't be here with me now if you didn't."

"Are you so sure of yourself, Michael McDonald?"

"I'm sure of one thing only, Adrianne, that I love you more than life itself. Let me show you all the ways."

"Teach me."

"With pleasure, my love."

Kate continued writing, bringing forth the sensual elements she was known for. As she wrote, it became harder and harder to divorce the words on the page from the images in her mind. Images of her, with Drew Buchanan. On the movie screen of her brain, she saw the pictures projected there, fresh, vital, erotic. Silken flesh against hair-roughened skin. Kisses skillfully played up and down the length of the woman's body; kisses so passionate she quivered in response. Feminine hands slowly touring a masculine form, lingering, teasing. Gasps and cries, sweat and tears, life and death, followed by glorious rebirth. Staggering sweetness. Complete bliss. Love.

Automatically saving the data, Kate took a break. Rising, slightly disturbed by her own musings, she stretched her taut muscles, rotated her neck. She needed a cool drink. Hell, or at the very least, a cigarette. Wasn't that the proverbial release after an especially invigorating bout of lovemaking? Trouble was, she didn't smoke, so she'd have to settle for the glass of iced tea.

Walking into the kitchen, she poured herself a refill, greedily drinking more than half the contents of the glass. Her throat was dry, her nerves raw.

She was an emotional writer, always had been. But tonight she'd been even more so, getting deeply inside her book. All because of Drew Buchanan.

He was inside her head, dangerously close to getting inside her heart, as well.

No way.

It was mere chemistry. Just that, she repeated to herself.

Kate walked back into the living room. She looked out the window when she saw the lights of a car pulling up toward the garage.

It was Drew. No mistaking that tall body as she watched him stride across the pathway and into the back of the house. Glancing at her watch, Kate was surprised to see him return for what she was sure was early for him. Barely past eleven.

She grabbed her purse and fished out a bar of dark chocolate from the interior. Tearing off the wrapper, Kate bit into the rich candy, sighing. As good as it was, it still didn't take her mind completely off the handsome Texan.

Nor did the songs the radio station played.

Damn. Why did the deejay have to play Bonnie Tyler's "Total Eclipse of the Heart"? Such a haunting song of pain and love, need and want. She listened to the raw emotionality of Tyler's voice; it never failed to move her.

She saw the flicker of a light in one of the upstairs bedrooms. His.

A sudden, intense yearning filled her.

God, it must be Bonnie Tyler night, Kate thought. She heard the familiar chords of "Holding Out for a Hero" play. Kate dropped her candy bar half finished onto the coffee table, moving closer to the window that faced the main house. He was up there.

And she wanted him.

Waited for him.

Without rhyme nor reason.

Could he feel the need? Could he sense the acute hunger that had sprung to life so unexpectedly?

Kate sighed, trying to rationalize the situation she found herself in. Loneliness. That had to be the lead factor.

She certainly didn't need a hero. Been there. Had one.

What she needed, wanted, was simply a man. A quick fix. Someone to help her through the night. This night.

It was all too crazy.

It was all too real.

* * *

She was still up. Drew could see the gleam of lights in the cottage below.

He paused, sliding a bookmark into place inside the paperback. He'd driven home from the party, anxious to get back to the book he'd started at Melanie's. Kate's novel. Normally, not his particular type of reading material. He favored nonfiction, biographies or political science, when he had the opportunity to read.

He'd been to Ireland, the setting of her romance. She'd captured it well, the spirit of the people, the cadence of the language, the incredible splendor of the scenery, giving her readers a strong sense of place. And, more important, of character. Drew felt that he knew these people. Knew what made them tick, what made them fall in love.

And he especially knew what made them want.

He could feel the same thing, sharpened to a razor's edge, eating away at him.

He'd have to have been made of wood not to empathize with the man and the woman she'd described, with their initial joy in discovering each other sexually. It was potently erotic, giving him a sense of what sex, in this instance, meant to a woman. Kate's details were intimate, her language pinpointing, emphasizing the mood.

Trouble was, he was in the mood. Exceedingly so.

A smile curved Drew's wide mouth. Truth of the matter was that he'd been in the mood since he'd first laid eyes on Kate Reeves. He was an itch waiting to be scratched.

Or so he told himself.

What harm would there be if he went down to check and see if she was all right? He would be polite, making sure she was comfortable.

Drew rose from his chair.

Screw polite! he thought as he flicked off the lamp. He *had* to see her. No two ways about it.

Mind made up, a confident look on his face, he went after his body's desire.

Chapter Four

Having returned to her writing, Kate was surprised by the knock that sounded on the door to the guest house.

Checking her watch, she saw that it was almost midnight. Quickly tapping the save command, she rose. As she made her way to the door, she felt the excited leap of her pulse.

Could it be him?

Only one way to find out, she thought. Open the door. She did so, discovering that she was right.

"Drew," she said, her tone slightly husky.

"I saw the lights on."

"I was working."

"Ever diligent," he mused.

"More of a case of I couldn't sleep."

His voice was low and seductive. "Neither could I."

Kate could end this right here and now before it went any further by telling him that she really couldn't be

bothered by company. Her writing was her top priority—
that was a viable excuse. She was right in the middle of
an important scene and had to get back to it.

She looked up into that handsome face. He stood
there, one hand casually resting on the doorjamb, a lazy
smile on his wide mouth, dark fires alight in his eyes.
"Come inside," she suggested.

Drew took her up on her offer, needing no arm twisting. She led him to the living room. His eyes followed
the soft sway of her hips beneath the cotton fabric of the
casual sleeveless slip dress she wore.

"Can I get you anything?"

Yourself, he mentally said. "What have you got?"

Whatever you want. "Actually," she said, "I was going to put on a pot of coffee. It looks to be a very late
night."

It could be, he thought. "Coffee's fine by me. I'm
easy to please."

"Are you, really?" she queried with an arch look.

Drew grinned. "I certainly can be under the right circumstances."

"Somehow," Kate countered, her blue eyes sharp, "I
imagined you'd be more demanding."

"Oh," he answered, his tone smooth as aged bourbon,
"I can be that, as well. Depends on what's being offered."

"Coffee."

Are you sure? he wondered. "Then coffee it is," he
said. *At least for the moment.*

"Make yourself comfortable, and I'll be back in a
minute."

"I'll be waiting."

She walked barefoot into the kitchen, her breathing
intensified. Oh, my God, Kate thought as she mechani-

cally went through the ritual of preparing the coffee. What have I done?

Time enough to back out. *I could tell him that I've changed my mind.* She scooped the coffee into the filter. *It's not too late.*

Who was she kidding? It was too late as soon as she opened the door and bade him enter.

No, even earlier than that her fate was sealed. It was too late when she first laid eyes on him, striding so confidently through the throng of people and chairs along the Paseo del Rio. Her body recognized the truth in that instant. A current so strong she was like a salmon swimming upstream to attain her goal. It couldn't be ignored. It could only be appeased.

Drew paced around the room as he waited for her to return.

He'd wanted women before.

Hell, he'd had women before; certainly his fair share. He'd never made a secret of liking their company, nor did he lead them on. He wasn't interested in marriage and happily ever after. At least not at present. A mutually satisfying relationship was more his style. Then, when it was over, he moved on. No regrets. No strings.

But he'd never met anyone who affected him as keenly as Kate Reeves did. This was *deeper* than he'd ever wanted. *Stronger* than he'd ever wanted. He was on fire for her. Hot. Searing. Burning completely to the core.

Kate could feel the heat from his eyes clear across the room when she entered. It scorched her with its warmth, piercing down to her very core. Her hands trembled as she carried the small wooden tray to the table, setting it down. "Coffee's ready," she said, moving aside her laptop and taking a seat on the small couch.

She glanced at the page on the screen before she flipped the lid down. Color flooded her cheeks. Had he read it?

As if he could hear her thoughts, Drew picked up one of the generous cups, poured in a splash of cream, then took a seat in one of the chairs. "No, I didn't invade your privacy, if that's what you're wondering."

Her eyes met his. "How did you know that's what I was thinking?"

"Good guess. I was tempted, believe me," he admitted freely. "It might have proved interesting to see what you were working on, but I couldn't do that to you without your permission. It's one thing to read a finished book. It's out there for all to see. Creating the prose is a different matter. Then, it's just you and the words, as it should be. Until you're ready to send it in to your editor, it's all yours and yours alone."

His admission, and tacit understanding of her writer's space, touched a responsive chord in Kate. "Thanks."

"None needed."

He was starting to complicate matters. Kate believed that she wanted whatever happened between them to be simple. Easy to rationalize and understand. Easy to put aside when it was over. She didn't want an affair with a man who was like an onion—so many layers to discover that one had to keep peeling to find the core.

"I beg to differ."

"Have it your own way." Drew shrugged his shoulders, placing his half-empty cup back on the tray. He held out one hand, palm up. "Dance with me."

Kate looked up. Without thinking, she put her cup beside his and rose, coming easily into his arms.

The radio, which she'd left on, was proving obliging. A slow, romantic ballad came over the airwaves, sweeping them up into its rhythm. As their bodies connected, Elvis poured out his emotion in "Can't Help Falling in Love With You."

Kate felt the warmth of his right hand around her waist; his left hand held her right tight to his chest as her left hand slid around his neck. The steady beat of his heart thrummed beneath her ear as she relaxed against him. They swayed, barely moving, neither noticing a few minutes later that the song had ended. His solid, big-framed body was pressed against hers, allowing Kate to feel the strength and passion it contained.

All hers for the taking.

She pulled back slightly.

Drew lifted Kate's chin with his right hand, his fingertips gently cupping her chin. His head descended, his lips capturing hers in a softly searching kiss.

Both of her arms went around his neck and pulled him closer. Kate went with her instincts, deepening the kiss, her tongue softly dueling with his, all else forgotten.

It had gone from mild to spicy in a heartbeat, Drew thought as he welcomed Kate's reaction to his kiss. There was no mistaking the hunger of her response. It was as potent as the Texas heat in summer, and just as hot.

He bent and swept her up into his arms, never breaking the kiss until he reached the stairs that led up to her bedroom.

"Tonight. This is for us," he whispered, his voice a low rasp of sound.

Us. The two of them, Kate thought as she clung to Drew as he ascended the stairs. As if in a fantasy, he was dramatically carrying her up, taking her into a new world where pleasure was the master, and she its willing servant.

No looking back, she realized. There was no past, no future. Only now. Only here. Only this.

He entered the room and put her down on her feet, then flicked on the light. Before they went too far, he had to make sure that this was what she wanted. He had no doubts.

"Tell me you want this as much as I do," he insisted, his dark eyes naked in their craving.

Kate couldn't deny the truth. "I do," she declared, her voice almost breaking. "Oh, God, I do."

Then a sudden thought struck her. This was embarrassing and awkward. "I...that is...do you...?" Damn! She sounded like an idiot.

"Protection?" Drew offered.

"Yes, that's what I was trying to say."

He smiled. He thought it was kind of sweet that she was slightly flustered. It was such a contrast to the sophisticated writer who crafted such sensual scenes of love. "Taken care of." Drew had slipped some foil packets into the pocket of his jeans before he'd left his room. It never hurt to be prepared.

He stepped out of the soft-as-butter brown Italian leather loafers he wore. Then he closed the small space between them, drawing Kate once more into his arms, seeking the sexual energy that he'd tapped into before. It was there, blazing hotter, growing stronger, feeding off itself until it threatened to consume them both in the conflagration.

Kate felt greedy. Greedy to have her hands on him. Greedy to have his on her. Greedy to make this night last as long as possible.

Her fingertips slowly slid up the wall of his wide

chest, clothed in a plain black T-shirt. That wasn't good enough. She needed to touch his skin.

"Take it off," she said, her voice husky with mounting desire.

Drew complied, releasing his hold on her to do as she wished.

Kate sucked in her breath when his naked flesh was revealed. Dark hair feathered across his powerful torso, arrowing down to his flat stomach, ribbed with lean muscle.

Her hands belonged there, stroking, learning all the contours. Jack's chest had been smooth and sleek, his body wiry. Drew's was bigger, broader, darker.

"My turn," he said. Before she knew it, Kate's dress was up and over her head, then tossed down on the carpeted floor in a heap. "Beautiful," he murmured huskily. "Much better than my meager imagination."

"You've imagined me undressed?" That idea pleased Kate.

"Since the first moment I met you," he answered honestly, sliding his warm palms up her back, over her shoulders, then through her hair. "Kate," he groaned, "I need your mouth again."

They kissed, long and lingering, accepting nothing from the other except total commitment.

It was like pouring gas onto an already surging, searing out-of-control fire. It went hotter, higher, deeper, threatening to consume them both in its wake.

They tumbled to the bed, rolling around and over, each grasping at the other, trying to get as close as they could, wanting, needing the ultimate closeness, the supreme forging of man to woman. Both sought shelter; both sought surrender.

Drew tore his mouth from Kate's, eager to explore her

further. He nibbled a path down her arched neck, inhaling the scent of her perfume until he found the valley between her breasts. He scorched her skin with the heat of his tongue as he dipped, stroked, laved, until moans of pleasure sounded from her throat. Sliding a hand behind her back, he unsnapped the closure of her lacy bra and removed it with her help.

Her breasts were perfect to his eyes. He cupped one, then the other, her creamy pale flesh filling his palm. His thumb scraped across a nipple; it puckered in response. Begging, it seemed to him, for his lips.

Kate bucked when his mouth closed over the nub, tugging on it gently.

It had been so long, and it felt so good, pleasure shooting through her at his touch. Her hands reached out and held his head to her body, encouraging him to continue. "Oh, Drew, don't stop," she whispered.

Drew didn't. He took it further, lavishing each breast with special attention while she ached, spiraling higher with each touch of his tongue. Tension was growing inside her, taking her closer to the edge.

He kissed her stomach, moving downward.

Kate thought she knew what was next.

She was wrong.

He bypassed the heat of her, heat threatening to explode at any moment. Instead, he brushed his lips along her inner thigh, around her knee. He lifted her leg, cupping the calf, feeling the smooth skin until he began to work his way back up again, moving closer to the core of her.

His eyes were dark and filled with desire as they met hers. Slowly, he exhaled, a dangerous smile on his lips.

She was going to die with want at any moment. She

could feel herself slipping closer and closer to the precipice.

It happened when his finger stroked a line from the edge of her French-cut briefs down, then slipped beneath the material, finding her.

Kate soared, her body like a rocket blasting off into space. She was out there, traveling the edges of the galaxy, then returning home, mission accomplished.

It had all been for her. Unselfishly, he'd seen to her enjoyment first, making sure that she reached fulfillment.

When she could form the words, Kate asked, "What about you?"

Drew gathered her in his strong arms, holding her close to his warm body. "Don't you worry about me, darlin'," he said, a satisfied smile on his face.

"But..."

He kissed her, his mouth capturing her words. When he raised his head, he said, "This time it'll be for us both. I promise." His smile was bewitching. "Remember what I said before. A Texan always keeps his word."

She watched as he rose from the bed in one fluid movement, her gaze narrowed as he peeled the jeans from his body.

Kate's eyes widened as Drew revealed all of himself to her.

It was her turn to smile.

He rejoined her on the double bed, his hands busy removing her remaining scrap of clothing, the cotton panties.

"I want you," he said, his voice a deep groan.

Kate pulled him to her, her short nails scoring his back as she held him tightly, clinging to him. He was so real, so alive, and he'd made her feel the same. It was as if she'd been in an enchanted sleep that had held her prisoner, locked away in the tower of her grief.

"Then have me," she whispered.

And he did, taking them both repeatedly over the top, keeping his word.

Kate thought she'd died and gone to heaven.

She smiled, contented, her body feeling deliciously satiated. She guessed that she had indeed knocked on heaven's door.

She was curled on her side, a pristine, albeit wrinkled denim-blue sheet tucked around her. Languid, she was reluctant to open her eyes. If it had been a dream, she didn't want to know. She wanted to lie there and savor the memories.

And what memories. Sweet. Intoxicating. Beautiful. Incandescent moments to hold in her mind, bright beacons of a total capitulation that Kate hadn't believed possible for her to feel ever again.

Following closely on the heels of those thoughts was another—guilt. How could she enjoy the act of making love? And it had been just that. Maybe not for him, but it was for her. She'd crossed the borderline somewhere, sometime during the night.

No, she told herself. No guilt. No recriminations. No second-guessing. She'd acted on instinct. On desire.

Whatever happened next, she would face it.

She turned over, hoping to see his face on the other pillow.

It was empty. So was the bed.

She brushed aside the solitary tear that had threatened to fall. Disappointment hit her, carving a hole in her stomach. A pit of emptiness that deflated her balloon of happiness.

It's not as if she hadn't actually expected it. There'd been no pressing reason for him to linger, really.

She just wished...

What?

That he'd have held her, been there with her when she woke up. That they could have made love again.

Greedy, aren't you? she asked herself.

Yes! He'd been an oasis at which she'd wanted to linger.

Was that so much to hope for? A respite from the lonely shell of widowhood, however temporary?

She glanced at the bedside clock. Morning would soon be here.

And then what?

Polite chitchat over breakfast with Emma? All the while, wishing that she were back in this bed, with Emma's formidable brother-in-law.

Kate heard a sound outside her door.

Could it be?

Happily, it was.

How was it, Drew wondered, that today, here and now, she looked better than any woman he could think of? He stood in the doorway, the wooden tray in his hands, just staring at her. Was it a trick of the lighting? Couldn't be. Or that wild mane of thick blond curls his fingers had tunneled through? Or was it that wonderful mouth he'd endlessly kissed?

Whatever it was, he wanted her with a surprisingly deeper appetite for having had so delicious a sample.

"Hungry?"

Kate pushed herself up and pulled the plump pillows behind her back, all the better to see him. And what a sight he was. Traces of dark stubble hugged his jawline. His hair was wavy, and one curl curved onto his wide forehead. A gold cross hung low in the whorling of dark hair that feathered across his chest.

"Starved," she replied, surprised to find she was truly famished.

"Good. Then these won't be wasted." He took the plate that was piled with assorted sandwiches and placed it on the small round table that was set off to one side of the large room.

Kate draped the sheet around her slim body and got out of the bed, padding over to where Drew had set up their repast. It trailed behind her like a train on a dress.

"Shame to see all that coffee go to waste, so I just reheated it in the microwave," he said as he held out one of the chairs for her.

She took her cup and took a hearty drink, enjoying the moment with him. It was then that she noticed the long, thin white scar that angled down from his shoulder to his upper forearm.

"What's that?"

"Souvenir of the time I rode a bull when I was thirteen. Needless to say, this particular bull didn't take to being ridden, and he tossed me a hellin'. Landed on my butt, and he came after me. Luckily, one of my friends managed to rope him before he did much more damage."

"Very dramatic."

"It was all in the name of a story." Drew picked up one of the generous sandwiches and helped himself to a big bite.

"A story? At thirteen?" Kate could well imagine the boy that he'd been. Tall, somewhat of a daredevil. Willing to risk injury for what he wanted. Brave. And foolhardly.

"Yep. For my school paper. I wanted to see how it

felt to be a bull rider, and I knew for certain that my father wasn't going to allow me to have a go at it, so I decided that I'd find another way.''

''Which you did.''

''And got in deep trouble for my efforts.''

Kate smiled. ''I take it your dad didn't approve?''

''You could well say that. I was grounded for a month, after I got a very stern lecture. I learned my lesson.''

''Did you?'' She wondered if that were true.

''Of course. The next time I wanted to do something like that, I made sure I had plenty of backup, and took precautions.''

''Do you do the same now that you're a journalist?''

He drank some of his coffee. ''It's not always possible.''

''So, you enjoy pushing the envelope?'' she inquired, biting into a ham and cheese flavored with spicy mustard.

''I don't know if you could call it that.''

''What would you call it? You obviously like living dangerously.''

''No, not always. A lot of the things I've written about are quite tame, I can assure you.''

''But you do like a challenge, don't you?''

He grinned, showing the top row of his perfect white teeth. ''Yeah, I suppose I do.''

''Is that what makes you take an assignment in a place like Bosnia?''

''Could be.'' Drew shrugged. ''I don't really stop to analyze why, I just go with my gut.'' He leveled a direct gaze at her. ''Don't you?''

He had her there. ''Yes, I suppose that I do. So,'' she

asked, after polishing off the sandwich, "what are you working on now?"

"Political corruption."

"Oh, something nice and safe."

"I don't worry about safe, sweetheart," he admitted. "All I care about is the story. Doing my job."

Doing my job. Jack had said that as well, on numerous occasions. He was just doing his job, trying to keep Philly's streets clear of the scum who terrorized innocent citizens. Protecting the weak from those that would prey on them.

"What's wrong?" Drew saw the flash of sadness that crept into Kate's eyes.

"Nothing."

"Nothing?" He didn't believe her.

"Really, nothing. I was just recalling someone else telling me something similar." She took another sip of her coffee.

Her husband, Drew assumed. None of his business if it had been. And he didn't want another man's presence in this room. Certainly not now. Adroitly, he changed topics. "What are you planning on doing today?"

Grateful that he chose not to pursue her last comment, Kate sighed in relief. "Emma mentioned maybe taking a drive out to the surrounding countryside. Maybe up to Kerrville. I'd like to see the area there, gather some research for a future book."

"Why don't I drive you?"

On one hand, Kate was thrilled that he wanted to spend more time with her. That their one night would hold over to the following day.

On the other, was it really wise to prolong her exposure to his Texas charm? Wouldn't it make it all the harder to leave on Monday morning, knowing that this time together was all there was to be?

"Let me check with Emma. I don't want to hurt her feelings. After all, I did come here to spend some time with her."

"Okay," he replied. "Do that. But if she has no objections?"

"Then I'd love to have you show me more of your Texas."

Drew glanced out of one of the windows. "It'll be daylight soon. I should leave here before anyone's up at the house."

"Yes," Kate agreed, "that would probably be best." But she didn't want him to go just yet. Hunger of a different sort clawed at her, demanding placation. She came slowly out of her chair, moving with a sensual grace toward the bed.

Emboldened, Kate raised her hand and unwound the sheet, letting it slide down her body. A smile on her mouth, she slipped onto the bed, feeling the heat of Drew's dark eyes on her. She certainly had his attention now, and she was determined to make the most of it.

"You don't have to leave just yet, do you?"

He inhaled sharply, the sight of her lovely body a temptation he couldn't, wouldn't, deny himself. Especially not after such a sultry invitation. He'd have to be made of stone to turn down such an appealing offer. "I think I can stay a little while longer."

Drew stood up. In seconds, he was beside Kate, his jeans left on the carpet in a heap, his mouth on hers, his hard body driving them both toward fulfillment.

She watched him leave. Standing at the French doors, Kate stared at his retreating figure as he made his way across the garden. Fingers of dawn slowly colored the sky.

It had been pure animal passion that had driven them this last time. As if they couldn't get enough of each other, they mated with everything that was in them. Wild and abandoned, just as it should be between lovers.

Lovers.

In the space of just over twenty-four hours her life had changed dramatically. Succumbing to passion's claim, she'd ridden the whirlwind of desire to its conclusion.

Or had the whirlwind ridden her?

Chapter Five

"Drew."

The soft female voice halted him just as he was about to take the stairs back to his room. He turned and nodded his head to acknowledge Emma's presence. Concern was clearly written on her face. "You're not going to lecture me, are you, Emma?"

She ran a hand through her tangle of short auburn curls and scoffed at the notion. "I wouldn't dare to presume to do that."

"Good."

Emma cautioned, "Just don't hurt her."

"I have no intention of doing that." Drew could tell that she was worried about her friend and hastened to reassure her. "Kate's a big girl. Old enough to know what she wants."

"You."

He couldn't prevent the smile that curved his lips at her pointed response. "It appears so."

"Don't start anything you don't mean."

Standing almost a foot taller than his sister-in-law, Drew looked down at her. "Do you think that it's any of your business, really?" It wasn't meant as a rebuke, merely a reminder of the fact that he and Kate were adults, each aware of the consequences of their actions.

"I feel responsible," she murmured.

"Why? Because you introduced us?"

"Yes, and because I wanted you two to get along," Emma admitted. "I thought you might be good for her. Get her..."

"What? Jump-started back into life?" Drew offered with a lift of one brow.

"Well, that isn't quite how I'd put it." Emma shot him a pointed glance.

He crossed his hands over his chest, head cocked to one side. "How would you?"

"It's just that I had hoped that if an attractive, single man took an interest in her, that she might like the attention. Remind her that she's still young, with a lot of life to be lived. I never meant to push."

"Kate's very much alive and knows what she's doing," Drew insisted. "There's no mistaking that."

"Do you like her?"

"What an odd question."

"Not really."

"Yes, I do," he readily admitted. "She's bright, funny, with a sharp sense of humor. And a keen brain. I've never been one for bimbos."

"That's thankfully a trait all the Buchanan men seem to share," Emma remarked sagely. "Speaking as an artist, Kate's an attractive woman."

"Very." Drew stifled a yawn. "I don't know about you, Emma, but I'm pretty wiped out right about now. I'm going to bed. Perhaps you should do the same."

"I am. I only came downstairs to get a drink of milk. When I heard the back door opening, I thought it was probably you." She went to the refrigerator and poured herself a large glass of cold milk.

"Is that one of Burke's robes that you're wearing?"

Emma smiled. "I miss him," she confessed, running her hands over the burgundy cotton as it hugged the swell of her stomach. "This makes it easier for me when he's not around."

"Oh my, you do have it bad, lady," Drew stated with a wide grin.

"One day it will happen to you, as well, Drew, and then I can say I told you so."

"Maybe someday," he said, giving her a fond peck on the cheek, "but certainly no time soon." Drew turned and walked up the winding staircase, calling over his shoulder, "'Night."

Emma stood below, watching him, a secretive curve to her lips.

Over coffee later that morning, Kate and Emma talked about the schedule for the day.

"I would really like to see more of the Hill Country if we could," Kate stated, refilling her large cup for the third time. After Drew had left her bed, she'd slept very little, so she needed the jolt of caffeine. "You know, take some pictures, get a feel for the area. I might like to set a book here, I think, and seeing as much as I can will be beneficial. That is, if it's okay by you."

"Actually," Emma said, "Burke called me about an

hour ago. He's on his way to San Antonio, and I'd like to be here to welcome him, if you don't mind?''

Kate leveled a fond glance at the other woman. ''I can certainly understand that.''

''I've also got a series of sketches that I'm working on for a show that's less than two months away that I'd like to go over.''

''Can I see some?''

''Sure,'' Emma replied, pushing back her chair. ''I left my sketch pad in the other room. I'll be right back.''

A moment after Emma left the kitchen, Drew entered.

Kate's face brightened upon seeing him. Her smile was genuine and heartfelt. She'd expected that this meeting might be awkward. Thankfully, it wasn't. It did, however, take all her considerable willpower not to jump out of her seat and fling her arms around Drew, greeting him with a big kiss.

Instead, with circumspection, she let her smile speak for her.

Drew read the message loud and clear, giving a careful glance around the room before he stepped up to her and kissed her quickly. '''Morning,'' he said, his deep, warm voice sending shivers down her spine.

As she watched him fix himself a cup of coffee, a sudden mischievous imp made Kate ask, ''Sleep well?''

Drew leaned back against the counter, taking a drink. ''Oh, I managed to catch a few winks here and there.''

''Restless?''

His grin was just this side of lascivious. ''Actually, I was having an episode of wonderful dreams.''

''Dreams?''

''Oh, yes,'' he said, lowering his voice, ''wild, wicked fantasies.''

''Really?'' she asked. Her gaze lingered on his wide

chest, covered in a smart, oatmeal-colored, designer-label linen shirt. He wore it with a pair of Levi's and the same leather slipper-shoes he'd worn last night. Her fingers itched to peel back that shirt, undo the buttons slowly, reveal that dark mat of hair beneath. She wanted to experience the texture with her hands, savor the taste of it again with her tongue.

"I've got it," Emma said as she entered, stopping in her tracks when she caught sight of the twosome. She recognized the rampant sexual tension that permeated the kitchen. It was real, and amazingly clear, especially to her artist's eye. These two radiated chemistry. Potent. Palpable. Purely sensational. The same kind she and Burke possessed.

"'Morning, Em."

"Drew." Emma took her seat, handing the large, hand-tooled leather book to Kate.

"What a wonderful piece of work," Kate said as she examined the careful designs on the cover and back jacket. Emma's initials appeared in fancy script, along with some Western motifs.

"A gift from Burke," Emma said proudly.

Kate flipped it open, looking at each page. Faces stared back at her; one in particular reappeared, that of Emma's husband. Several more were of a young girl Kate knew was Jessie Buchanan. A handsome couple in their early fifties graced a few pages, along with numerous landscapes. "Is this the Buchanan ranch?" she asked.

Drew came to stand over Kate as she stared at the images before her. "Yes," he answered before his sister-in-law could. "Em does a wonderful job in capturing it in all its many phases."

Kate felt her pulse leap at his nearness. She also

caught the scent of his aftershave—rich, woodsy and definitely masculine.

"Can I quote you on that?" Emma asked teasingly.

"Of course you can, darlin'," Drew stated, reaching over Kate's shoulder to place his hand over hers as she paused on another black-and-white sketch.

Kate felt the tingle clear through her, vibrating with a life of its own.

Drew felt it, as well. He smelled the clean, crisp fragrance of her shampoo. Floral. Like a garden of earthly delights. Her hair shone a golden color, with streaks of paler strands. He longed to plunge his hands into it again, molding her scalp while his mouth plundered hers.

He wanted her! Here. Now. If only they were alone, he'd show Kate just how much. So much that he ached with holding it in.

Kate Reeves was temptation. No doubt about it. Utterly irresistible temptation.

His only regret was that this affair would be over all too soon. That by tomorrow she would be out of his life.

He moved away from her, giving himself some space, though keeping her within sight.

Easy come, easy go.

No, he reckoned, not always.

"Drew, Kate wanted to see some of the Hill Country. Do you have some time today to play tour guide again?"

His answer required no thought. "Be my pleasure."

Emma refrained from making a comment in response to that statement. "Is that all right, Kate?"

"Sure." As if she would turn down a chance to spend time alone with him. Not likely!

"Do you have any place in particular you want to see?" Drew asked.

"What about Kerrville?" Emma suggested. "I've been there before, to see an exhibit at the Cowboy Artists of America Museum. There's plenty of other things to see around there. Burke took me and Jessie on a ride around some of the historical sites while we were in the area."

Kate smiled. "Sounds fine to me."

"Then I suggest, if we're gonna make a day of it, we get a move on soon," Drew added.

"Great." Kate rose. "Just give me a few minutes to get my camera and a few other things." She addressed Emma. "Your work is terrific, as usual. Are you planning on using some of these in the exhibit?"

"I thought that I might. These are some roughs. I'll go through them and decide which ones to enlarge. Normally, I do paintings, oils or acrylics. This exhibition calls for pencil or charcoal."

Kate wished she had the guts to ask for a simple drawing of Drew. But she wouldn't. Besides, she had a feeling that Drew's image was already locked away inside her brain and that she wouldn't need an actual physical reminder of him. Her memories would be sharp enough.

Drew shifted as he watched Kate quickly finish the remainder of her coffee. When he could pull his eyes away from her, he checked his watch. "Meet you outside in ten."

Kate sliced him a teasing glance. "Be there or be square."

"Burke wants us all to get together for dinner tonight," Emma said as Kate was about to walk out the back door. "Somewhere fancy. So make sure that you're back here by seven-thirty or so. That should give you plenty of time for your *adventure*."

Kate paused, her hand on the antique glass doorknob.

She had the distinct impression that Emma was saying more than she actually was. Did her friend suspect that she and Drew had been together last night? And if Emma did know, what did she think? And why hadn't she said anything to Kate over breakfast when she'd had the chance?

"More than enough," Kate stated, closing the kitchen door behind her and walking outside, crossing the garden. She stopped to smell the roses, feeling unexpectedly happier than she had in a long time, deciding to put needless worries aside for the moment. It wasn't that she was unhappy; just that today there seemed to be a special joy to her mood.

She knew who and what was responsible.

Drew Buchanan was the who.

Great sex was the what. First-rate, world-class. The kind that put a smile on your face and a fire in your belly, demanding more of the same.

Kate breezed into the guest house, ran up the stairs to her room, gathered up the items she'd need for her trip and tossed them into a handy tote. She added extra film, checking on what was left in her camera. She wanted pictures, her own visual diary of this trip.

By the time she made it downstairs, Drew was waiting for her, the Jag's engine purring.

Emma walked Kate to the black car. "Have a great time."

"We will," Drew assured her, reaching over and flipping open the door for Kate.

She sank into the expensive leather and fastened her seat belt. Reaching into her tote, she pulled out her camera, aiming it in Emma's direction. "Smile," she ordered.

Emma did, and Kate snapped a quick photo before Drew maneuvered the car out of the driveway.

He quickly got onto I-10 West, heading for Kerrville, the Jag eating up the miles.

Drew sliced a glance at his silent companion. She, like him, was wearing sunglasses to protect her eyes from the hot Texas sun. A black baseball cap sat perched on her thick tumble of curls, emblazoned with the logo of the latest James Bond movie. A deep rose T-shirt hugged her curves, tucked into a pair of white cuffed shorts. Her long, slim legs were smooth and bare. He recalled the heart-shaped birthmark high on her inner right thigh; his lips had kissed it, his fingertips had traced it.

His hand tightened on the steering wheel.

Taking his mind off its dangerous path, he pushed in a tape and music flooded the car.

"You're into rock 'n' roll, aren't you?" Kate asked, tilting her head and drinking in the sight of his strong profile. He had a timeless face—the kind one found stamped on coins, sewn on tapestries, painted on frescos or carved in marble.

"Love it," he answered, adjusting the volume when Bob Seger's "Old Time Rock 'n' Roll" came on. Drew sang exuberantly along to the music, his left hand beating out a steady tattoo in time to the beat.

Time and distance sped by, until Kate saw a sign that indicated Kerrville was near.

Drew pulled his car off the next exit, following a single-lane country road.

"I thought the next exit was ours," she asked, curious as to why he was leaving the interstate earlier than necessary.

Slowing the Jag down, he pulled it over to the side of the road. "You want to know why?" he asked, sliding his right arm along the back of her seat. "So that I wouldn't have to wait any longer to do this," he murmured in that sexy drawl.

He held Kate in his arms, his mouth on hers, solidly convincing her of his true purpose.

"That answer your question?" he demanded softly, his eyes looking deeply into hers.

"I think you may have to repeat it."

He did, making his point even stronger.

Kate felt like a giddy teenager, necking recklessly with her first boyfriend, alone and uncaring of the rest of the world. She loved Drew's kisses, surrendering to the warmth and passion with equal fervor, giving back as good as she got.

Drew reluctantly withdrew from their heated embrace. It was either that or he was going to suggest something totally crazy right here out in the open. His body was clamoring for hers, forcibly straining against the fabric of his jeans.

He took a deep, steadying breath and turned the key, starting the Jag's mighty engine. It revved to life instantly as he pulled back onto the highway.

Music filled the silence between them for a few minutes until Drew spoke. "There are plenty of things to do and see in the Hill Country," he explained. "See that gate over there?" Slowing down, he pointed to a large stone-and-iron entrance. "One of the many dude ranches you can find out here."

"No kidding?" she asked. "Where they take city slickers and give them a chance to experience the West?"

"Exactly."

"What a hoot."

"An expensive hoot, I would say," Drew said dryly.

"It's all top-notch there. Not your average dude, believe me. More like doctors, lawyers, stockbrokers. That sort." He grinned. "They wouldn't last two days on the real thing. Burke would eat them alive."

"I can believe that."

"There are others that are less first-class, but give you what you're looking for. A working ranch."

"I'm sorry that I won't get to see yours while I'm here."

"It's not mine," he said.

"Well, your family's, same difference."

"It'll be Burke's, and he's welcome to it."

"You don't want it?"

Drew answered her question honestly. "I'm not a rancher. I love the place, sure, how could I not? I grew up there, and it's in my blood sure as it's in every Buchanan's. But as for wanting it, no, that's not me."

"Don't you live there?"

He shook his head. "Nope. I've got a room there, whenever I want, which, according to my mother, isn't often enough."

"Where do you live, if you don't mind my asking?"

"San Antonio, mostly, when I'm in Texas, at the family house. However, I like traveling, having the chance to see other places. I love the northern coast of California, the wild beauty of the Rockies, the hospitality of the South and the bustling pace of New York."

"But you don't feel attached to one certain area?"

"Not at present." He reached out and grabbed her hand, giving it a gentle squeeze.

"I love where I live."

"Tell me about it," he coaxed.

Kate didn't have to have her arm twisted. "There are gently rolling hills—horse country. It's quite beautiful, really. I lived in Philly when I was married, in a town house in Old City. Jack, that was my husband's name, was required to live in the city since he was a cop, so after we got married, we moved to a lovely old place. He was originally from South Philly. I was from the suburbs. We'd always talked about having a weekend place outside, far enough away so that we'd be in the country, away from the stress of urban life, but close enough for friends and family.''

Drew listened to the softly spoken words, heard the underlying wistfulness there.

"When I began to do well with my writing, actually getting our dream was becoming more of a reality. I found a wonderful place for us, and we had a great time picking out house plans, going over catalogs for garden stuff. Jack loved gardening. It was going to be our retreat.''

"And now it's yours, isn't it?'' he asked.

"Yes. Mine alone now. Jack never lived to see it finished.'' Kate was quiet for a moment. "He would have loved the way it looks now. It's a place for roots. Permanence. I love traveling, too, but I'm always glad to come back to my own home. I like knowing that there's something waiting for me, in addition to my dogs.''

"You've got dogs?''

Kate laughed. "Have I ever. Two collies. Maverick and Iceman.''

"Excuse me?''

"You heard right.''

Drew snapped his fingers. "I get it. *Top Gun.*''

"It was one of Jack's favorite movies—mine, too. When we saw those pups, one tricolored, the other golden, I couldn't resist calling them that. We bought them right then and there. The names fit.''

She had a life, he thought, one she was anxious to get back to. Roots, she'd said. The one thing he wasn't really looking for at this stage in his life. She was a woman for the long haul. He was a man for the moment.

They'd visited the Cowboy Artists of America Museum, which Kate learned that Drew's family supported; later, they walked around town, then strolled through some of the old cemeteries outside the city limits. All the while, Drew watched as Kate chatted with people, her easy manner winning even the reluctant over. She jotted down notes, took endless photos. Her canvas tote bulged with souvenir brochures, postcards, books and magazines.

On the way back to San Antonio, he'd stopped by a gas station that also had a small shop attached. While he filled the tank, Kate went inside.

Behind the counter, a big-boned woman fanned herself. She smiled in Kate's direction. "That's some fancy car your husband's got hisself."

"My husband?" Kate realized that the woman had noticed her wedding band and logically assumed that Drew was her husband.

Before she could correct the woman's misinterpretation, the woman spoke again. "We don't see too many like that around here. You just passing through?"

"Yes." Kate went to the refrigerated compartment and removed two large bottles of ice-cold spring water. Her mouth was so dry, she couldn't wait to down a few hearty swallows. She put the bottles on the counter and added two big candy bars for good measure. It was then that she spied a small, spin-around wire rack, crammed with paperbacks. Unable to resist, she gave it the once-over and found one of her earlier titles.

Grinning, she picked it up. "Do you mind if I sign it?"

The woman looked at her suspiciously.

"It's mine, I swear it," Kate avowed, pulling her driver's license from her tiny canvas handbag to show the lady.

"Henry. Come in here." The woman called for her husband.

The late-middle-aged man strolled in, mopping his furrowed brow, his overalls worn and slightly stained with old grease spots. "Yeah, sweet pea?"

"We got us a real celebrity here, we do. It's one of them writers."

Drew walked in, watching the scene from the doorway, a wide grin on his face.

"Would you sign it 'To Millie'?" the woman asked, beaming at the pleasure of having an honest-to-God published writer in her establishment.

Kate smiled. "It'd be my pleasure." She took the pen the woman held out to her. "Do you read romance novels?"

"I like to read, period, honey," the other woman answered. "As long as it's a good book that I hate to put down, I don't care."

Kate autographed the copy. "I hope that you like it, then."

"I'm sure that I will," Millie promised. "I'll start it today."

"My address is inside. Drop me a line and let me know, will you?"

Millie was flabbergasted. "You want me to tell you what I think?"

"Of course."

"You won't be disappointed," Drew assured the woman.

Kate shot him a surprised look.

"Bet you must be right proud of her?" Millie asked.

"Busting my buttons, ma'am," Drew responded, playing the role of happy partner to the hilt as he paid for the gas.

"Why, you're a Texas boy, aren't you?"

"Yes, ma'am, I most certainly am."

"You've also got good taste, honey," Millie addressed Kate. She looked Drew over. "Mighty good taste, indeed. No one holds a candle to a Texan. They're the best," the woman said with pride, adding, "then there's the rest."

Drew swallowed the laugh that threatened to leap from his chest at that blunt remark.

Kate picked up the paper bag with her items. "They're something else," she responded. "No doubt about that." She walked past Drew to the door. "Ready, Tex?" she asked over her shoulder.

"Be there in a minute, darlin'." Drew smiled.

He was enjoying this, Kate thought as she walked to the car, removing one of the bottles and twisting off the cap. She took a drink, the cool water sliding down her parched throat. Next, she unwrapped the candy bar and bit into the chocolate-covered caramel-and-nougat center, sighing.

"I've got something for you."

Kate spun around at the sound of his voice. "What?"

"Hold out your hand and close your eyes."

"My mother warned me about taking gifts from strangers."

"We're hardly strangers," he teasingly reminded her. She lifted her chin, her eyes meeting his. "Guess you're right, there.'' She put the bottle on her seat, along with the half-eaten candy bar, then held out her hand and closed her eyes. A small object touched her palm.

''Okay, you can open them now.''

Kate looked down. There, nestled in her hand, was a cloisonné lapel pin of the Lone Star State.

Her eyes lit up; her smile deepened. She rose on her toes and gave Drew a tender kiss on his cheek. ''Thank you.''

''It was nothing,'' he said. ''A little trinket. I thought it might be a fun souvenir of the day. A reminder of our outing.''

She immediately fastened it to her shirt. ''I don't have anything for you.''

He totally disarmed her with his response.

''You gave me the pleasure of your company, Miss Reeves. That was more than enough.'' Drew opened the door for her, waving to the couple as they stood under the awning of their building.

''Well, I did get you something,'' she said, handing him the extra bottle of water and candy bar.

''You shouldn't have,'' he demurred mockingly.

''The least I could do.'' Kate looked at him, threw caution to the winds and grabbed his face in her hands, planting a big kiss on his lips, to the delight not only of the couple watching, but more important, to her own delight.

''Do that again and we might not make it to dinner,'' he said with a growl.

Kate sat back and fastened her seat belt, a wicked smile on her face. ''There's always dessert.''

Chapter Six

Dessert was all Drew could think of as he dressed for the evening to come. Visions of the woman in the guest house floated in his mind; tantalizing glimpses of anticipatory moments with the beautiful Kate.

He selected his wardrobe carefully, uncharacteristically anxious to wear something that she would find pleasing.

Kate Reeves.

He recalled, vividly, the feel of her hands skimming across his chest, her silken touch driving him wild. The brush of her thick blond hair across his shoulders, along his arms, tickling his stomach.

He remembered the way her body quivered with each stroke of his hand, each touch of his lips. To embrace her was like holding quicksilver. There was so much passion locked deeply inside her that the revealing of it

almost sent him reeling. She was so natural, so uninhib-
ited. Divinely, deliciously female to the core.

She was one special lady, no doubt about that. And
she was his for only one more night.

Tomorrow their paths would divide; she would rejoin
her own world, he'd return to his. All that would be left
were memories. Sweet souvenirs of an interlude permeated with magic. Unbelievable magic. And pulse-
pounding chemistry.

An affair to remember.

Impulsive. Wild. Abandoned.

Kate had never really thought of those words in connection with herself before. However, after this weekend, she knew she'd have to revise her thinking,
somewhat. How else to explain her chuck-caution-to-
the-winds attitude when it came to a certain charismatic
Texan?

She hadn't held anything back when they'd been together. She'd given and taken in equal measure, until it
wasn't possible to take or give anymore. All the way—
plumbing the heights and depths—that's how she'd responded.

There was only tonight. One last chance to grab the
brass ring. Tomorrow, sanity would return. Tomorrow,
she'd willingly return to her life, gather up the memories
and go on. This had been a weekend out of time, caught
momentarily in her palm like grains of sand.

But what memories they'd made together. Sweet,
spicy, special. The caress of his hand, the feel of his
lips, the smell of his skin, the thrust of his powerful
body. All this and more combined to reawaken her slum-
bering senses, making her come achingly alive again.

Tonight she would wear something special. It was an occasion and deserved the one outfit she'd packed for a fancy evening.

Kate went to the closet and examined the dress she'd recently purchased. Yes, she decided, a smile on her mouth, this would do very well indeed. He ought to like this. Sophisticated and smart, it said *female*.

That was an understatement.

Heat slammed into Drew's body when Kate walked into the parlor of the main house. He and Burke had been sitting, chatting about family matters, enjoying a tall glass of iced tea when she made her entrance.

Both men rose from their chairs.

Drew let his gaze slowly wander from the top of her nimbus of golden hair to the high-heeled sandals she wore, lingering on the way the material of her dress, a clingy knit of deep teal, molded her body. It shaped and hugged, like the hands of a lover, leaving plenty of her long, sexy legs visible. She wore an intricate, Celtic-design sterling-silver-and-amber brooch.

"Irish?" Drew asked, stepping closer to her. The temperature in the room had risen, he was certain, by at least twenty degrees.

"Yes," Kate acknowledged, her heart beating rapidly. "It was a gift from my husband on our honeymoon."

Drew brushed aside a lock of her hair, his fingertips caressing the lobes of her ears as he examined the matching earrings. "He had good taste." Softly, he whispered for her alone, "In so many things."

"I like to think so," she replied, her eyes meeting his. God, she could willingly drown in the depths of those dark orbs. Funny, she'd never been one much for chocolate-syrup brown eyes before. But there was something she saw in his; something she couldn't ignore.

Now it was her turn to admire him. Drew wore a fancy black dinner jacket and trousers, a crisp white shirt and burgundy tie. He looked as though he'd just stepped out of an ad in *GQ*. Perfect. One hundred percent male. So damnably good-looking and sexy it hurt. If his younger brother hadn't been in the room with Drew, Kate would have walked right into his arms.

"Hi, Burke," she said, tearing her gaze away from Drew and extending her hand. "How did your daughter do in her event?"

A proud smile curved Burke's wide mouth as he returned her greeting. "She placed second in the junior division. We're all quite proud of her."

"As well you should be," Kate stated. "That's great for her first competition. I've been to a couple of the Devon Horse Shows and seen some of the young riders there."

"We could have a future Olympian in the family," Drew commented, escorting Kate to a seat on the low leather couch while they waited for Emma.

"That's up to Jess," Burke replied, giving a careful glance to the body language of the couple. They were sitting close together, Drew's arm around the back of the couch, near Kate's shoulder. Each was having a hard time keeping their eyes off the other. Emma was right, he decided. Something was definitely going on there.

"Have you enjoyed your stay with us?" Burke inquired politely.

Kate wet her lips. *If he only knew.* "Very much."

"Perhaps you'll come again? I know that Emma would like that. And next time, we'll make certain you come to the ranch."

Kate wondered if that would be possible, letting
Burke's offer go unanswered for the present. If Drew
wasn't involved, then she might consider it. When she
left tomorrow, she had to put him out of her life, out of
her mind. He didn't want involvement, nor did she; especially not with a man for whom work proved occasionally dangerous. She'd been down that road before,
with dire consequences. Never again.

"Are we ready?"

All assembled looked to the doorway where Emma
stood, a glowing smile on her face.

Burke leapt to his feet, joining his wife. He slipped
an arm around Emma's waist, one hand resting casually
on her swelling abdomen. "Just waiting for you, darlin'," he murmured.

"Then," Emma invited, "let's go, shall we?"

The hotel where they were having dinner was beautiful. Old World charm mixed with sophisticated culi-
nary style. It catered to the movers and shakers, many
of whom, judging by the traffic their table was receiving,
appeared to know the Buchanans.

Kate sat back and enjoyed the meal, even the occasional interruption. She watched as Burke and Emma
took any excuse to touch or gaze longingly at each other,
or to make a private joke. She secretly wished that she
could do the same with Drew, but that would be tanta-
mount to flaunting her affair with the older Buchanan
brother, and that wasn't part of her makeup. What she
and Drew had was between them, private. There was no
room for confessions or recriminations. Kate didn't want
it to be a problem when she was gone.

"Would you care for dessert?" the waiter asked, indicating with a neat nod of his gray head to another staff

member that the silver, four-tiered rolling tray was to be brought to the Buchanans' table.

Dessert, Drew thought. Slowly removing Kate's clothes, lingering over each item, drawing out the tension until she was totally revealed; that was his idea of a tempting item with which to top off a magnificent meal.

Dessert. The taste of her lips, flavored by champagne. Dollops of whipped cream, strategically placed and licked off. Strawberries dipped in warm chocolate, drizzled over certain areas and then used for edible decorations. His mouth was watering. He doubted that anything like that was on the menu.

Dessert. Something cool and captivating, Kate thought, like the way Drew smiled. Hot and tantalizing, like the way he kissed her mouth and touched her skin.

Dessert. Taken at leisure, savoring every single mouthful, with all the time in the world for enjoyment. Or, voraciously satisfying the hunger quickly, gratification demanding an immediate response. With Drew Buchanan, Kate could well imagine both.

She licked her lips, staring at the multilayered cart. "Everything looks delicious. I don't know what to choose."

"Then let me," Drew offered.

Kate turned her head, tilting it at an angle, gazing deeply into Drew's eyes. Her smile was her acceptance.

Emma gently poked Burke in the ribs, making sure he took note of what was happening.

"Something chocolate for the lady," Drew announced, surveying the choices. "This, I think." He pointed to his selection.

It was dispatched immediately and placed before Kate. "And for yourself, Mr. Buchanan?"

"The same."

The waiter chuckled. It was the hotel's own version of Demise by Cheesecake. "Mrs. Buchanan?"

Emma sighed. "Nothing quite so decadent, Henry. The Dutch apple pie will be fine."

Burke added, "Same for me."

Drew grinned at his brother and sister-in-law, a devil-may-care look. "No guts, no glory."

Kate paused, her fork halfway to her mouth, a bitter-sweet memory tugging at her heart. Jack used to say that very same thing.

Drew saw Kate's momentary hesitation and asked, "What are you waiting for?"

Kate smiled in his direction, recovering her mood, putting the past behind her. "You." She delivered the line with aplomb.

"Well, darlin', you're in luck. The wait is over." He clicked his fork against hers in a salute.

Simultaneously, they tasted the treat.

Kate sighed in pleasure after the first mouthful. "You're a very wicked man, Mr. Buchanan," she admonished.

His eyes sparkled. "You bet."

"This is wonderful," she said, taking another forkful. "It tastes like authentic, rich New York-style cheesecake."

"That's because it is." Drew laughed. "The hotel hired the chef away from a great little bistro in Tri-BeCa."

Burke raised one dark brow. "What my brother isn't telling you is that he insisted that they hire the woman."

Kate sliced Drew a direct glance. "You did?"

He demurred. "I thought that she'd make a great addition to the staff here, so I suggested that if they were interested in a terrific pastry chef, I knew one who might be available.''

''And they hired her?''

Drew nodded. ''All they had to do was have a sample of her work.''

Burke added pointedly, ''My brother always did have a way of getting whatever he wanted.''

''Not all the time, little brother,'' Drew protested.

''Just about.''

''And what haven't you gotten that you've wanted?'' Kate asked, sampling another bite of the dessert. Right now, she knew what she wanted. To be eating this marvelous concoction curled up in that big brass bed at the guest house, Drew by her side, one fork between them.

Drew considered the question. What did he want?

Kate. Right now. Alone. Soft lights. Music.

And time. All the time in the world to discover what she was about. Enough hours in the day, and night, to sample all the ways they could make love.

He delivered the more prudent answer. ''An exclusive interview.''

''With whom?'' she asked, fascinated.

When he named several deceased political figures of the past two centuries, Kate was impressed. This tall Texan was not just another pretty face. He had style and substance. An intoxicating, seductive combination. One she was finding more and more irresistible.

Impossible! In less than twenty-four hours they'd resume their separate lives, close this chapter and move on to the next.

Every minute counted. She couldn't sit there any longer, playing at being convivial when what she wanted to do was be with Drew. Completely.

''I hate to break this up, but I do have an early flight

tomorrow morning," Kate said, hating the fact that she was making such a flimsy, paltry excuse, but she couldn't help it.

"Yes," Emma agreed, "I suppose we should get you home so that you can go right to bed."

Kate almost dropped her fork at Emma's remark. That's exactly what she wanted, but for a far different reason than what she thought Emma expected.

The mood was mellow on the quick ride to the house on King William Street. Kate sat in the back seat with Drew, their hands linked, an occasional heated glance exchanged.

Drew felt like a schoolboy, eager to be alone with the girl of his choice, away from prying eyes. Yet it wasn't with a youth's callow fervor to get a sexual itch scratched that he wanted Kate. It was the mature yearning of a man for a woman, encompassing all the depth of his past experience. Plain and simple.

Drew knew that this was just an affair; neither of them was looking for a long-term thing, but, atavistically, he wanted to make his mark, stamp his possession so solidly that Kate Reeves wouldn't be able to forget this particular Texan anytime soon.

Why?

He couldn't answer his own question. He hadn't a clue as to the underlying motive. All he understood was that he wanted her. And want was a good enough answer for now.

His hand was warm and strong, enveloping her much smaller one, their entwined digits a symbol of what was to come. Tremors of excitement ran helter-skelter through Kate's system. Anticipation heated her imagination, flushed her cheeks. How long would it take before he could join her? Minutes? An hour? Longer? Good things come to those who wait. Or so it was said.

He would come. He had to. One last night together before the future beckoned. Later, she would try and make sense of this. But not tonight. Tonight was for loving, for being caught up in the fantasy, for riding the tiger.

"What time's your flight?"

Kate snapped out of her reverie to answer Emma's softly spoken question.

"Nine."

"We'll take you to the airport," Emma said, "then we can leave for the ranch from there."

Drew squeezed Kate's hand. "I can see that Kate gets to the airport if you'd rather take it easy in the morning."

"It's no trouble..." Burke started to say, when Emma nudged his thigh with a gentle poke of her left hand. He shot her a swift glance and recognized the determined look in his wife's eyes.

"Yes," Emma decided, "that might be better all around, if you wouldn't mind, Kate? I've got a few calls to make regarding arrangements for my next show in the morning. Always details to work out."

Kate couldn't hold back the deep smile that brightened her face. A reprieve of sorts. She'd get to spend at least a bit more time with Drew. "Do what you have to, Emma," she replied. "I'd be happy to accept your brother-in-law's very kind offer."

"That's settled, then," Emma acknowledged as Burke pulled the car into the drive.

As they walked through the garden, Emma and Kate stepped apart from the men.

"I certainly hope that you've had a good time while you were here," Emma inquired.

"The best."

Emma wanted to say that she suspected that a large part of that was due to Drew, but she bit back the remark. Kate would, if she wanted to, tell her in her own time about her involvement with Drew. Until then, Emma would keep what she knew to herself. However, she couldn't help but think that they made a rather handsome couple. Striking, the pair of them.

"I'm going to miss you," Emma confided.

Kate stopped and hugged her friend. "And I'm going to miss you. This time's gone by way too fast."

"Don't I know it."

"And I want you and Burke to come and visit me sometime. You know you're always welcome. I'd love to show you guys around my part of the country."

Emma patted her stomach. "Maybe after the baby's born."

"Whenever. Or, if you're in New York, give me a call. It's only a train ride away for me, you know."

"Okay."

"Guess this is goodbye, then." Kate hugged Emma again. "Thanks for asking me to come. I needed this break." *In more ways than you can imagine, dear friend,* Kate silently verbalized.

Emma blinked back the moisture in her eyes. "I've found that for some people, Texas takes a piece of their heart." She looked in Burke's direction. "For me, it was a very large piece. Coming here changed me for the better. I'm a lucky woman, Kate—I've got it all—my career, an expanded loving family and, most important, Burke's love. You once advised me to reach out for the happiness that I wanted because one never knows how long it may last. I did, and I've never regretted it. Think about that advice, my dear. It's not too late.''

Kate inhaled, tears forming in her eyes, as well. "I hear you.''

"Do you?" Emma smiled, kissing Kate on both cheeks. "I hope so.'' She took a deep breath, plunging ahead. "Remember, your marriage vows said 'until death do you part.' It's Jack who's dead, Kate. You're not. He wouldn't want you to be alone the rest of your life. From what you've told me, he loved you too much to wish that for you. So, tell me that you'll think about what I've said.''

Kate swallowed the small lump in her throat. "I will.''

"Good.'' Emma smiled. "Now, knock 'em dead on the rest of your tour. Sell tons of books.''

Kate laughed softly. "From your mouth to God's ear.''

Burke sauntered over to where the two women stood. "Drew said that he'd see you tomorrow, Kate. He had some things to take care of before he turned in.'' The tall, lean Texan slipped his arm around Emma's waist, a gleam of hunger in his dark sloe eyes as he asked in his husky baritone, "You ready, darlin'?''

Emma sighed, momentarily leaning back against her husband's solid chest, her head resting on his shoulder. "You betcha, cowboy.''

Burke leaned over and kissed Kate on the cheek. "Take care, and come on back,'' he repeated his earlier invitation, "anytime. Friends of my wife are always welcome to the Encantadora.''

"Thanks, Burke. I appreciate that.'' Kate glanced at her watch, just barely reading the correct time by the amber outside lights left on. It was almost midnight. A secret smile curved her lips. Tomorrow, Drew said. "Guess I'd better turn in, too. 'Night.''

It was a warm evening, perfect for leaving the French doors of her bedroom open to catch the breeze. Maybe she'd even sit on the balcony in that old wicker chair and watch the stars. The night sky was beautiful. A midnight blue, freckled with dots of sparkling silver-white. There was a bottle of white zinfandel chilling in the refrigerator. Kate contemplated a glass or two of that while she waited.

Perfect. All she needed to make this complete was the man himself.

Checking the time on his watch, Drew hastily removed his formal dinner clothes and tossed them onto a nearby chair, pulling on a clean pair of black jeans and a black T-shirt.

Damn! He was running late and he didn't want to keep Kate lingering much longer. A blinking answering machine signaled calls, a few of which he had to return as soon as he could. Leads and contacts for his upcoming article. In his line of work, business often took precedence over pleasure.

But tonight?

He slid his feet into a pair of casual black canvas shoes. Satisfied that he'd taken care of everything, he chanced a glance from his window toward the guest house. It was dark, except for the lights from her bedroom. Drew thought he spotted a figure on the balcony but he wasn't sure.

Then he saw movement.

Yes, it was Kate, leaning on the railing, a glass of something in her hand.

Drew inhaled deeply, as if he could catch the scent of

her gardenia perfume from across the distance of their two houses.

Smiling, he picked up the phone on his desk, punching in the number of the cottage.

He watched her move through the open doors, back into the bedroom.

"Hello." Her voice was soft; it flowed like warm honey over his senses.

"What are you drinking?"

She gave a throaty laugh. "Wine."

"Have you saved some for me?"

"I've got more than enough here for you."

"Oh, you do, do you?" he asked with a husky chuckle.

"Why don't you come over and find out for yourself?" Kate licked her lips, deriving pleasure from this not-so-subtle game of questions. Hearing his voice was better than nothing; but what she wanted was him, here, in the flesh, right this minute.

"Is that an invitation, Ms. Reeves?"

"I'd say it's closer to a blatant request, Mr. Buchanan."

"Then, how can I refuse? I'll be right there."

"Hurry."

Kate hung up and strolled back out to the veranda. She picked up the bottle of wine from the Waterford ice bucket, pouring him a glass.

She sat down, crossed her legs, an anticipatory smile kicking up the corners of her mouth.

Less than a few minutes later he was there, walking up the side steps. She held out a fluted glass, also Waterford. Her eyes did an inventory of his body as he stepped closer, mentally tallying every element of his personal style. He was all in black—like a midnight fantasy. The shirt hugged. The jeans caressed. Dark desire personified.

Drew quickly drank half the contents of the wineglass and put it down on the small round table. It was Kate he wanted to taste. Kate he wanted to imbibe. She was all the stimulation he required.

When she went to refill his glass, he stopped her with a softly uttered command. "Later."

Kate raised her eyes to his, welcoming the inevitable. Her arms went around his neck as he picked her up, carrying her into the bedroom.

He groaned, setting her down and wrapping her securely in his arms. "Do you know how difficult it was sitting in that restaurant when what I really wanted to do was be alone with you?"

Kate pressed tiny kisses along his jawline, his cheek, the strong column of his throat. "Since I was feeling the same, I think I do know how hard it was."

They looked into each other's eyes, seeing the truth of their mutual attraction. Like a fire gone wild, gathering heat along the way, their passion burned.

Unnecessary clothes were shed.

Hungry kisses were exchanged.

Sweet love was made.

In the darkness, Kate lay with her head pillowed on Drew's wide chest. The flaw in her hastily drawn plan to have an uncomplicated weekend affair was now evident, in spades. She cared for this man. Deeply.

But it was over.

It had to be. He wasn't right for her. Not for the long-term. This was an indulgence. A temporary retreat into never-never land that had to end. She'd told herself that she could handle the take-no-prisoners attitude of an affair.

Obviously, she acknowledged, she was mistaken.

Drew wasn't a man a woman casually put aside or easily dismissed. He made an abiding impression.

The very thing Kate didn't need. She wanted easy, forgettable, no strings. No mess, no fuss. A chance encounter that served the purpose. Something that she could walk away from, the same way she knew he'd walk. Two strangers who'd met, touched, communicated, then went on with their respective lives. It worked well in theory.

She inhaled the scent of his skin, her fingers feathering across his flat stomach. In so short a time, his body had become familiar territory to her. She knew where to touch to drive him over the edge.

She'd gone with her gut, reaching out for the pleasure he offered, thinking that she could handle the consequences. Situations like this happened all the time. Just not to her.

Would he believe her if she were to tell him that he was only the second man she'd ever made love with? She'd been spoiled with Jack. As a lover, her husband had been wonderful.

It looked as though she'd been spoiled again. Drew was extraordinary. In his arms, she'd felt reborn. Renewed. Shown the way back from the valley of the shadow.

But it was time to let go. Move on and store this in the memory box of her mind, where it belonged.

Kate shifted, and when she went to get up, a masculine arm stopped her.

"Where are you going?" His voice was sleepy, and far too sexy for Kate's peace of mind.

"To take a shower."

"Sounds like a good idea." Drew tossed back the sheet, standing up.

Kate watched the ripple of muscles in his back, blushed when she saw the faint marks of her nails. "Together?"

Drew turned around, a major-league grin on his face. "We take water conservation very seriously here, ma'am," he drawled.

She put aside her wistful thoughts and returned his smile, holding out her hand for his. "Far be it from me to stunt your environmental efforts, Mr. Buchanan."

The airport was crowded with early business travelers. Kate's flight had just been called.

"Guess this is goodbye," she said, gathering her carry-on bag and purse. She wanted to ask him to go before she made a fool of herself. She was so damned afraid that she would cry at any minute. What did you say at a time like this? *Bye. Been nice sleeping with you. Have a good life.*

"I wish you luck on the rest of your tour."

"Thanks." She moved into the line of fellow passengers.

Drew stood beside her, unable to break the connection. In minutes, she'd be on the plane, gone. It didn't seem right. They'd been so calm and cool since they'd entered the airport, almost like strangers. This wasn't the way to end it.

"Wait."

"What?" she asked as several passengers boarded.

Drew gently tugged on her arm, pulling her out of the line.

"Drew, I've got a flight to catch," she protested.

"I know. You won't be late, I promise. It's just that I couldn't let you go just yet. At least not before I've had a chance to do this." He gathered her into his embrace and kissed her. "This doesn't have to end, you know," Drew remarked, slowly removing his lips from hers.

Kate blinked in surprise, hardly noticing the people pushing past her, eager to board the plane. Oh, but it did, she thought, pain fisting in the region of her heart. It had to—for her peace of mind. Right now, she couldn't handle what he was surely offering, a continuation of the past few days. And, as wonderful as they'd been, Drew Buchanan was still who he was, an untamed Texas maverick who wasn't the type to settle down, to want to hear the words she longed to say.

Kate had already, she suspected, lost her heart. She'd be damned if she'd toss in her pride, as well. "I'm afraid that it does."

Dark eyes bored into hers. "Why?"

She reached up her hand, gently brushing aside the curling lock of hair that fell across his forehead. Tears welled and she fought them back, determined to remain cool and calm. "Because it's over."

"Only if you let it be."

A bittersweet smile curved her lips, lips that still carried the imprint of his. "Why prolong the inevitable?"

His mouth kicked up into a sensual grin. "I can think of plenty of reasons, darlin'."

"If push comes to shove, I'm sure that I could too," she stated, hearing the last-call announcement as it came over the PA system. "But they wouldn't really change a thing. You're who you are, Drew. I'm who I am."

"What's that supposed to mean?"

Kate hefted her flight bag onto her shoulder. "Only

that it was nice while it lasted. Let's leave it at that, shall we?''

"Can you?"

I have to. "Yes."

He stared at her, trying to read the truth in her face. "Okay," he said, accepting her words. "If that's the way you want it."

"It is." Kate took a deep breath, giving him a fond smile. "I've really got to go." She turned around, ticket in hand, heading for the gate.

"Goodbye, Kate."

She paused for a second, looking over her shoulder, watching him as he turned and strode down the corridor, without so much as a backward glance.

Kate stood there, momentarily stunned as people moved around her. Her fingers touched her slightly swollen lips.

Taking a deep breath, she squared her shoulders and boarded her flight.

He hadn't gone far, only to the nearest bar a hundred yards or so away from her gate. From his seat next to the window, Drew watched her plane take off. He raised his tall glass of iced tea in salute. "Take care, darlin'," he murmured.

Chapter Seven

"You can't stop thinking about him, can you?"

Kate took a sip of the chilled white zinfandel her sister-in-law Mariah had just poured. "Is it that obvious?"

Mariah answered, "It is to me."

"You know me so well," Kate replied.

"It isn't so hard to figure out, Kate. You've been different since you came back from that book tour. It changed you, or—" she paused, taking a drink from her glass, her silver heart charm bracelet jingling "—should I say *he* changed you. You miss him terribly, don't you?"

"More than I thought I would," Kate acknowledged. "Much more."

"I don't know why you'd think that," Mariah admonished, "because casual isn't your thing. You're an all-or-nothing kind of woman. Always have been, always will be."

A buzzer sounded from the kitchen.

"I'll be right back." Mariah walked into the other room, leaving Kate alone with her ruminations.

Yes, she couldn't get Drew Buchanan out of her mind. Waking, sleeping, working, he was there with her constantly. She wanted him still, more so with each passing day. This was no ordinary want, much as she pretended it had been. It wasn't casual, or commonplace, easily forgotten once they'd been parted.

Memories of their time together haunted her, deeper and stronger with every dawn.

Mariah was right. Chance sexual encounters weren't her thing. But she hadn't been able to resist the temptation to succumb to the primitive pull of the senses that Drew awoke in her. It was greater than mere sexual hunger. She recognized that after they were first together. She'd pretended then that she could have a fling with a man and think nothing more about it, other than having desires met and satisfied. Happened all the time. Needs to be fulfilled; expectations to be met. Keep it light and without complications. Go with the moment.

The moment had come and gone, and so had her illusions. She was in love with him. A love that Kate hadn't believed it was possible for her to feel again. When Jack died, she'd thought that her capacity for love, that special kind of soul-connecting love, had died also.

Drew Buchanan had proved her wrong.

"Drew." She spoke the name aloud with wonder.

Kate relived some of the passion of their encounter while writing her latest book. Snippets of her sensual recollections wove into her narrative, dredging up the powerful intensity she'd felt that weekend in his arms.

She'd come back home determined to keep that time as separate from the rest of her life as she could muster.

That resolution hadn't lasted very long.

The first thing Kate did was surf the World Wide Web until she found a listing for the magazine he worked for, scrolling through until she found some of his work on file there. She'd downloaded copies of his articles, reading through them, discovering that Drew was, in fact, quite a good writer. Thoughtful and thought-provoking, his prose captured and illuminated whatever the topic was with insight and clarity. He made complex issues understandable by focusing on the people caught up in the chaotic swirl of events. Even the lighter pieces he'd done were wonderfully crafted portraits of the subjects.

Brains, talent, humor and sex appeal. A most compelling combination of ingredients for a man. Jack and he shared those traits, along with one she'd noted before—a sometimes offhand disregard for danger, for the ugly realities of their worlds, as if they were somehow above the fray.

The day Jack was killed, his guardian angel must have been stuck in traffic. So far, Drew's was still on duty. Kate could well imagine that he'd occasionally pissed off people with what he wrote about on certain topics.

Jack had fought corruption and evil with reason and a badge. Drew fought it with passion and a pen.

Jack Terrelli had loved her.

Drew Buchanan didn't.

Kate had no illusions about that score. It was she who'd fallen into that trap.

"Dinner's ready," Mariah called out, popping her head around the door frame.

"Coming," Kate replied, rising from her comfortable seat in the living room of Mariah Terrelli's Old City town house, three doors up from where she and Jack had lived when they were married. Kate walked into the small dining room, which was aglow with light suspended above the polished mahogany table. Her sister-in-law's taste was a bit more formal than her own, but it was worth it. Mariah preferred the elegant charm of the Victorian era, and her tastefully furnished home reflected that. In the age of greyhound-thin, waiflike models, Mariah was a throwback to the Victorian days when women were appreciated for their hourglass shapes.

"When do you find the time?" Kate asked, sitting down to a delightfully served meal. A large platter of hot spinach pasta was on the table, along with a large bowl that contained a sauce of fresh tomatoes, basil and garlic. Hot, crusty Italian bread sliced thick and a tossed green salad completed the dinner.

Mariah shrugged her shoulders. "I like to cook, so I make the time," she explained. "Having company gives me an excuse to indulge. Besides, it relaxes me, and after the day I had today, I needed it."

"Tough case?"

Mariah gave a deep sigh. "Very. Neglected children. Rampant abuse. Unfortunately," she said, a sadness in her tone, "it's becoming more and more the usual."

Kate admired Mariah's determination to improve the lot of children. Her sister-in-law was a lawyer for a prestigious center-city firm, but spent a lot of time doing pro bono work with children.

"Did you win?" Kate picked up the silver server and loaded her plate with pasta, ladling the sauce on top and adding freshly grated Parmesan and Romano cheeses.

"I like to think so. Time will tell." Mariah poured more wine into her glass. "The parents are in jail and the kids are in a much better environment, with good people to care for them. But," she insisted, "I don't want to talk about me. It's you I want to hear about."

Kate twirled the pasta around her fork. "What do you want to know?"

Mariah fixed the other woman with a sharp glance. "About *him.*"

Kate chewed her food carefully before she answered. "What about him?"

"Have you gotten in touch with him?"

Kate shook her head. "No."

Mariah's heavy bracelet jingled again. "Why not?"

"Because that wouldn't be a good idea."

Mariah gave Kate the same kind of look she would if she were questioning her in a courtroom—thoroughly penetrating. "Would you care to elaborate?"

"It was just an affair."

"Not for you it wasn't."

Kate sighed. "You know that and I know that. He doesn't."

"Don't you think he should?"

"It's not Drew's concern." Kate picked up a slice of bread and tore off a chunk, staring at it as if it contained all the answers.

"Concern? That's a rather stiff word to use, isn't it?"

"Not necessarily."

"Get real, Kate. You fell for this guy. What's wrong in letting him know?"

"You would, wouldn't you?"

"Yes," Mariah replied, "I probably would, but we're not talking about me and what I'd do. You're evading my question."

Kate knew Mariah wouldn't give up. "Because he's not interested."

"Well how the hell would you know that if you haven't said anything to him?" Mariah rolled her pale gold eyes. "Is he supposed to be a mind reader? Or is he an operator for a psychic hotline in his spare time?"

Kate laughed softly at Mariah's wisecrack. "Not hardly."

"Okay, then. He might be interested."

"If he was, then he knows how to get in touch with me." Kate took another forkful of pasta into her mouth, chewing it slowly before she continued. "He hasn't. That's good enough for me."

"Maybe he's respecting your space?"

"I don't think that's the case at all, Mariah. Drew's a very sophisticated man. This wasn't his first foray into an affair, and I'm sure it won't be his last. I was just one in a long line of women eager to be with him. Nothing special."

"Don't sell yourself short, Kate."

"I'm not. I'm merely being realistic."

"When you told me about the affair after you came back, I was glad, you know."

"You were?"

"Yeah. I thought it meant that you were finally putting Jack's death behind you and getting on with your life." Mariah's face took on a more serious look. "I loved my brother very much, and I know without a doubt that you did, too. You two had something special, something that so far seems to have eluded me in my relationships," she confessed. "I envied you, until I saw what his death did to you.

"Then, when you confided in me and told me about the wild weekend when you did the nasty with some hunky Texan stud, I was happy. Everyone deserves the kind of fantasy lover he proved to be. The kind that you write about in your romances. The type we'd all like to find knocking at our door, even if he, God forbid,'' Mariah said with a smile, ''ate crackers in bed.''

Kate started to snicker.

''What's so funny?''

''You made me remember a certain fantasy I had about him and a dessert we were having.'' Kate described the cheesecake and where she wanted to eat it.

Mariah joined in the laughter. ''Honey, you are wicked, which is what I like about you. So, he's the man you'd invite into your bed to share a fabulously decadent dessert. Doesn't that tell you anything?''

''That I have some imagination and an oral fixation?'' Kate replied with a smile.

''Not just that,'' Mariah laughed again, ''though you do. You wanted to share experiences with him. Most of all, you wanted to share yourself. If this Texan's half the man you said he is, then he should have realized how special that made him.''

''I don't think that Drew thought of it in quite that way. What's so distinctive about being just another woman he's slept with?''

''Because,'' Mariah observed, ''it was *you* that he slept with. He didn't make you feel like a number, did he?''

''Of course not,'' Kate protested. ''A number? No way. Drew's too classy for that.''

''Then, why are you being so hard on yourself?'' Mariah probed, digging into her dinner before it cooled.

''Because I thought I could handle what an affair entailed. I wanted him. Desperately. It was like being hit with a shot of adrenaline. When he strode through that crowd of people, smiled and offered his hand, I thought I'd been smacked—what's the expression?—upside the head. Drew got my attention right then and there. I could barely take my eyes off him.

"And then, to recklessly consider sleeping with him. It was all too crazy. Irrational. Not like me at all."

"Yet you went with your instinct."

"I had no other choice," Kate explained.

Mariah offered, "You could have said no."

"Perhaps. But I didn't want to. I thought there'd be no harm in it. We were almost strangers, not likely to get complicated. It would be simple and safe. It wasn't as if I were picking up some faceless guy in a bar and taking him back to my hotel room for a quickie."

"Heaven forbid in this day and age."

"Isn't that the truth. With Drew, I felt both free and safe. I was so drawn to him. He left the decision up to me and I made it."

"And," Mariah declared, "he was good in bed. That was a big plus."

"Good," Kate stated honestly, "doesn't quite cover it. Drew was wonderful. Beyond my expectations. That's the problem."

Mariah raised an auburn brow. "Excuse me?"

"The only other lover I've had was your brother. What Jack and I shared was very special."

"That's obvious to anyone who ever saw you two. But what has that got to do with you and your Lone Star Lover?"

"I thought what went on between us would be all physical. You know, just good sex, and that would be that. I hadn't counted on falling for him, or finding out that he was so much like Jack in so many ways."

"Like Jack?" Mariah asked, curious. "How so?"

"Guts. Integrity. Dedication to his work, and a predilection for danger." Kate explained further about some of Drew's articles, giving her sister-in-law a brief version of some of his stories, especially the incident in Bosnia. "So, even if he were interested, he's not the man for me. I can't go through that again, Mariah, wondering and waiting for the phone call to come. I won't."

"Fair enough, I suppose."

Kate tilted her head, staring at Mariah while the other woman calmly ate her dinner. "Then you understand? God knows that I don't sometimes."

"I think so." Mariah took another drink of her glass of wine. "You're afraid."

"Afraid?" Kate paused, resting her chin on her overlapped hands for a moment, considering the other woman's words. "Well, I wouldn't put it like that. I'm being quite logical about this."

"Logic doesn't have a damn thing to do with this and you know it," Mariah stated calmly. "It's all about control."

Kate looked perplexed. "Control?"

"Yes," Mariah insisted. "As a writer, you're in control of the world you create."

Kate interrupted her. "Not always, believe me."

Mariah smiled. "Humor me. Technically, you're in control, manipulating events and characters, getting them to tell a story. Like a popular mystery show, the murderer always confesses in sixty minutes, less commercials. All neat and tidy. Would that life were really like that. Unfortunately," Mariah added, "it isn't."

"I know that."

"Then you must know that you're drawn to this man because he represents your quintessential hero, like Jack did. Or so you said. Falling in love with him was, I'd say, pretty natural for you."

"And foolish."

"Because you fear that, like Jack, he could be taken from you abruptly, so better you don't give him a chance in the first place."

Mariah could have also made her living as a shrink if she'd wanted to, Kate thought. "We had the only chance we were supposed to have, that weekend."

"How can you be so sure?"

"I would think that's obvious."

"He could be shy."

Kate chuckled at that notion. "Not hardly."

"Well, from all you've told me about him, I didn't really think so, but one never knows."

The phone in the kitchen rang.

"Are you going to get that?" Kate inquired.

"I'll let the machine pick it up," Mariah said, until she heard the loud male voice asking if she were there would she please answer.

"Damn, it's work. I've gotta take it."

"No problem," Kate assured her.

Mariah got up and walked into the other room while Kate sat finishing the remains of her meal, thinking over what her sister-in-law had said. Most of it made sense.

Should she have pursued him? Should she have phoned, faxed or E-mailed him?

Or was she smart to keep her distance, ignoring the growth of the feelings she had for him? Love wasn't part of the unspoken bargain that they'd exchanged that weekend. Mutual need, mutual want. That's what they'd had. All that they'd had. Anything extra was only on her part, she was certain. If he'd wanted to, he had only to ask Emma how to get in touch with her. Or he could have written her. It wasn't as if she were totally incommunicado, not with her address in the back of her books for readers' mail, and an address for an on-line service.

He could have sent flowers. Called her publisher. Hired a detective. Anything. *If* he wanted to.

But there hadn't been one word from him. Nothing. It had been what it was—a short-term affair of a few days' duration, no biggie in his life, obviously.

This was her problem. Drew hadn't asked her to fall in love with him. On the contrary, he'd been up-front, never lying. No words of love had ever passed his lips. Sex, yes. Passion, definitely. But love, no.

Actions had consequences. Kate knew that. She'd willingly chosen a course and followed through with it. Taken a chance. Tossed the dice. Played her cards.

She wouldn't be the first woman to want what she couldn't, or shouldn't have. Nor would she be the last.

"Sorry about that," Mariah said as she reentered the dining room. "It was one of the other partners."

"Nothing serious, I hope."

"It depends. We're handling a private adoption and the clients want to make sure every *i* is dotted and every *t* crossed."

"I'm sure."

"So it makes for some last-minute questions and arrangements. I may have to fly out west and check on everything there in a week or two."

"Where out west, if I'm allowed to ask?"

"Montana, of all places."

"I've heard it's beautiful out there."

"Yeah, but with their weather, I'm liable to get snowed in for weeks. Yuck." Mariah took a taste of her salad, giving Kate a sharp glance. "I wonder what the weather's like in San Antonio about now?"

"You're not going to give up, are you?" Kate asked.

"Why should I?"

"Because my relationship with Drew is a dead issue."

"I don't think so."

"Well," Kate answered, "I know so."

It could never really be dead for her, Kate thought as she entered her kitchen, greeted by the two dogs. "Miss me?" she asked as she bent down and ruffled their gleaming coats, letting them show her with yelps and licks that they had. She'd told her sister-in-law a half-truth at best.

Hanging up her coat, she put on the kettle to heat water. The temperature was chilly outside, a fine autumn night. Stars were plentiful, as they had been on that last night in San Antonio.

Damn! She didn't want to think about him anymore tonight. It was all Mariah's fault, bringing it up and not letting it go.

Wrong.

She'd been thinking about Drew Buchanan all day—and every day since her return from that book tour. She couldn't honestly pretend otherwise.

Kate poured the now boiling water into a large mug of hot chocolate. Her second of the day, but who was counting? She needed the comfort of chocolate tonight, warm and sweet. After that dinner and conversation, she was wired, too wired to go to bed. Better that she put this energy into either her work—perhaps she could get another couple of pages done on her latest—or surfing the bulletin boards.

A few minutes later, comfortably attired in her over-size navy blue sleep shirt and knee-high thick wool socks, Kate flipped on the light to her office, mug of chocolate in hand. She turned on her laptop, and there was an indication that mail was waiting for her. Relaxing in her chair, she sorted through her messages, making a copy of the letter from her editor regarding a change in the last manuscript that she'd turned in. Another note was from her agent about an upcoming writers' conference at which both were speaking.

Kate cruised through the rest, answering a few of the notes from close friends in her inner circle, those who were part of a private chat room, and then reading comments from readers about her work.

It was the last entry in her box that stopped her. A brief message from someone. She checked the log-on name, which meant nothing to her, then read the brief message.

"No man is an island."

What was that all about?

Kate reread the short communique. Was this someone's idea of a joke?

Oh, well, she decided, it wasn't worth worrying over. She had work to do, so she clicked on to the chapter she'd been writing today.

Bad idea.

All it did was reinforce the memories she wanted to bury, dredging up images of her and Drew, together, intimately entwined. Kate closed her eyes, shutting away the words, letting the impossibly sweet mind pictures take over. She heard the husky, whispered conversation; felt the powerful movements of his body; responded to the tender ministrations of his hands as they cupped and stroked; melted under the barrage of sugar-and-spice kisses he bestowed.

It was like turning on a videotape in her mind, letting it play back endlessly the scenes that were her personal favorites.

God, but she honestly loved Drew Buchanan.

Kate opened her eyes and looked in the direction of

a silver-framed photograph on a shelf above her head. *I never thought I ever could, or ever would, love like this again, Jack,* she thought as she stared at the man in the photo. *Once in a lifetime. Not many people get that. I did, and I was the better for it. But twice?*

And at what price?

Even if I could, I can't.

She'd led with her heart before, and paid for it, even if loving Jack had been worth it.

Sometimes lightning struck twice.

Kate shivered. That's what she was afraid of.

Chapter Eight

"Something troubling you?" Burke Buchanan asked of his older brother Drew, putting a hand on the other man's broad shoulder. "You seem a million miles away."

Not so much a million, Drew thought, as several thousand. The distance from his family's ranch in the Hill Country to wherever it was in Pennsylvania that Kate Reeves lived.

"It's nothing," Drew replied, gazing across the expanse of land from his vantage point beneath a spreading live oak, staring at the gently rolling hills of the property, watching as horses frolicked in a nearby paddock.

"Now, if I were to say that to you," Burke insisted good-naturedly, "you'd tell me, 'Bull, I've got eyes in my head, and I know my brother all too well to fall for some lame excuse like that, especially when I know it's an outright lie.' Am I right?"

Drew's wide mouth curved into a smile as he turned his head in his sibling's direction for a momentary acknowledgement. "Guess you've got me there, Burke."

"Damn straight I have," he insisted. "So, what's wrong?"

"Am I that obvious?"

Burke cast a quick glance back at the crowd of people that milled around the area where they'd set up tables for the christening party for his infant son. It was a warm day in October, the weather cooperating wonderfully for the event. "Maybe not to everyone here, but like I said, I've got eyes. So, tell me. I'm here for you, you know," he declared, "just like you were for me last year when I was going through my personal crisis."

"And that certainly turned out well, didn't it?" Drew asked, recalling the dilemma Burke found himself in, falling in love with his older brother Clay's girlfriend. "You've got yourself a terrific wife, a wonderful daughter and a brand-new son."

"I'm a lucky man," Burke conceded, a once-rare smile curving his mouth. "Damned lucky, and I know it."

"That you are, little brother."

Burke put his hands in the pockets of his dress jeans. "So let me return the favor, won't you?"

"What say we take a little walk, then," Drew suggested, "away from the familial throng. Okay?"

"Sure."

The two brothers strolled toward the paddocks, Burke calling over his brown-and-white paint stallion and feeding the animal a few carrot sticks from his palm.

"So, does this have anything to do with a woman?" Drew reached out his hand and stroked the horse's neck, the well-brushed white mane hanging smooth and unfettered. "You could say that."

"What about her? Who is she?"

"I met this woman months ago," Drew began. "No big deal, I thought. She was interesting and we got along fine. She was passing through the city, on a business trip, so there was no real need to explain that I wasn't interested in a long-term commitment. Apparently, she wasn't, either."

Burke's voice was low and neutrally pitched. "Did you sleep with her?"

"You know me, Burke. I like to grab the bull by the balls, so to speak."

A chuckle escaped Burke's lips at his brother's salty comment. "I gather then that it was a memorable experience."

"You could say that, since I haven't been able to forget it. Night after night, day after day, she's there, in my mind, a part of me, like living tissue grafted onto my own skin. I'm hardly a novice with women, but there was something different about this woman, about being with her. A richer, deeper feeling of communication between us. Nothing held back. No barriers. No games. Just honesty, and the ultimate expression of the passion we shared.

"I don't want to be trite and sound like something from a supermarket tabloid headline and say it was the best sex I've ever had," Drew confessed, "because it was more than sex, at least more than anything I've known." He leaned his arms over the tall wooden fence. "It was hot, burning with an intensity that I hadn't thought possible.

"I've never wanted a woman as much as I did her. I had to have her."

"And you did." Burke inhaled deeply. "What you hadn't counted on was how much it would affect you?"

"Exactly."

"Sounds serious to me," Burke replied. "Have you gotten in touch with her?"

"I told you, I didn't think she wanted anything more from me than that time we spent together."

"But you're not sure?"

Drew shrugged his shoulders. "No, I'm not."

"All you do know is that you want more."

"Damn straight," Drew answered. "I want as much as I can get."

"What's stopping you?"

"Habit, I suppose."

"What the hell is that supposed to mean?"

"That I'm not used to wanting this way, little brother," he admitted. "In the past, I've called the tune. Love was a game and I played by my rules. Something to enjoy as long as it lasted, then, when it was over, I walked away. No second thoughts. Now, for the first time in my life, I want to look back. I want to have second thoughts. It's pretty friggin' crazy, I know."

"Not so crazy, *mi hermano*," Burke said, gazing toward where his wife sat, their son snuggled comfortably in her arms. "I'd say that you're in love."

"That thought had crossed my mind. Many, many times in these past few months."

"It's Emma's friend, Kate, isn't it?"

"How did you know?"

Burke gave his brother a get-real look. "It wasn't a challenging mental leap to make. I simply put two and two together and came up with a couple. Something happened between you and Kate Reeves while she was in San Antonio. I can recognize the signs of mutual interest in a man and woman. Between you two, it was evident, believe me. Maybe not so much that first night, but by the time I returned from Jessie's riding event and we went to dinner, I figured things had progressed. There was a sense of intimacy."

Intimacy. He'd been intimate with women before, but intimacy brought to mind a deeper connection; it implied a bond of some sort. Drew slanted a glance at his brother. "Yet you didn't say anything?"

Burke shrugged. "You're both adults. What was between you was your own business. I figured if you needed someone to talk to, you'd consider me. I may not have as much experience as you in dealing with women, but I'd give it my best shot."

It was Drew's turn to reach out and grasp Burke's corduroy-covered shoulder. "Thanks. Do you know what the hardest, the most surprising thing, was for me? To let her go. Pretend that what we shared didn't mean anything to me out of the ordinary. When I drove home from taking Kate to the airport, I kept thinking that I could have said something to her. I could have asked her to stay. Or to come back. I could have rearranged my schedule so that I could be with her. But I realized that I couldn't."

"Why not?"

"Because then I would have had to admit that she meant something to me. Something beyond the other women who have been in my life. And I wasn't ready for that."

"And you are now?"

Drew paused for a moment. "I think so."

"Then," Burke inquired, "what are you going to do about it?"

"Contact her."

"I think that's a good start."

"If I don't, Burke, then I won't be able to live with myself. I'll always wonder if there was something there to build on and I let it slip away, and that's not the way I like to live my life."

Burke remarked, "Seems just like the advice you gave me last year. Glad to see that you're gonna take your own words to heart."

"Do you know if Kate's said anything to Emma?"

"If she has, Emma hasn't told me. And," he stressed, "I won't ask her to betray a confidence if Kate has."

"No need to," Drew insisted. "Besides, coming home to attend this party, I wanted an excuse to talk to Emma myself. She knows Kate."

Burke's protective instinct for his wife kicked quickly into gear. "She's not an information source for one of your articles, Drew. Remember that," he warned.

"Don't worry, little brother," Drew said, understanding his brother's attitude completely. A Buchanan looked after his own. It was part of the family motto, learned while in the cradle. "Emma's family, and I wouldn't do anything to screw that up." Drew tapped Burke on the shoulder. "Looks like Mama's waving us back. Must be time for the cake cutting or something."

"I suppose. We've already opened most of the gifts. I may need to add an additional wing to the house to store them all."

"Did I see one from the White House?"

Burke smiled proudly. "Yep. An antique toy."

"Your son really is a great-looking boy, with all the natural Buchanan charm. He's got all the females wrapped around his tiny finger. One sweet smile and they're tripping over themselves to do his bidding. And I think that Dad's happy as a pup, as well."

"He and Mama are going to spoil him silly," Burke stated, "as will Jessie. She dotes on being the older sister. I give credit to Emma for that. She made certain that my girl didn't feel left out in any way, and when she asked Jessie if she could legally adopt her, well I thought Jess would burst from sheer joy. Now she can finally have what she never did before, a *real* mother's love. Someone who'll be there for her."

Drew concurred. "Best thing you ever did besides marrying Emma was to pay your ex to stay out of Jessie's life."

"Don't I know it?" Burke agreed.

As they walked back to where the crowd was gathered, Drew asked, "I assume that Kate was invited?"

"Yes."

"Do you know why she didn't come? I had sort of hoped that she'd be here."

"Scheduling conflict, I think Emma said. Some writer's thing Kate had to go to. Speaking of which, now that you've finished that exposé of political corruption, what are you working on?" Burke inquired. "Planning on something else equally explosive?" This was a sly referral to the slew of indictments that followed the piece when it ran in the magazine.

"Actually, I'm working on an idea that is a little closer to home."

"What?"

"A biography of sorts."

"Of who?"

"Our ancestors, Tory and Rhys Buchanan."

Burke considered his brother's words.

"So, what do you think?"

"An article wouldn't do them justice."

"I'm well aware of that. That's why I talked to an

agent, to see about putting the idea to some of the publishing houses in New York.''

''And what did he say?''

''*She* said she loved the idea and would give it a shot. I did up a quick proposal, then faxed it to her.''

Burke laughed. ''I stand corrected. Have you talked to the folks about it?''

''They gave me their blessing. You know how proud they are of those two.''

''As are all the family.''

''So, you're okay with the idea?''

''Fine by me. At least I know that the writer will get his facts straight and do a good job. I wish you luck. There's a lot of stuff here at the ranch, some in San Antonio and more in storage in safe deposit boxes. I expect the English branch of the family has some items that might prove useful, too.''

''I've already contacted our cousin there. If it goes through, which I expect to hear soon, then I'm taking a leave of absence from the magazine and going to work on the book full-time.''

''There you are,'' stated Santina Buchanan, the matriarch of the Buchanan family, a stunning woman in her mid-fifties, looping an arm through each of her younger sons'. ''We thought we'd lost you somehow. It's time to open a few more presents for my grandbaby, then cut the cake. It's right that his daddy and godfather are here to be witnesses.''

Both men laughed. ''Yes, Mama,'' they said in unison.

They were joined by their older brother Clay when Santina left them to rejoin her husband, Noah. Strikingly handsome in his sweater and chinos, Clay and his siblings made a fine picture of Texas manhood. Each man tall; each man distinct. Brothers to the bone—Buchanans to the soul.

"How about a couple of shots of the entire family," the photographer called out, assembling the people as she wanted them. "Move a little to the left, would you?" she demanded of Clay. "And you, tall in the saddle," she added with a laugh toward Drew, "move to the right. Yeah, that's it." She adjusted the lens of her camera, checking the light and moving back and forth, up and down, getting just what she wanted.

"Who's she?" Clay demanded softly.

Burke replied, "Someone Drew knows."

"Oh." Clay shot his brother a look. "And how well do you *know* her, Drew?"

Drew sliced the oldest Buchanan brother a withering glance while his family guffawed at the suggestion. "Well enough to know that she'd do a great job, and that's about it. She's someone I met through the magazine. Just an acquaintance. Why?" he asked. "Are you interested?"

"Could be."

"Then go for it."

"Thanks for your blessing," Clay stated wryly.

"Ready everyone?" the photographer called out. "Let's do it."

"Yes," Clay added softly, a smile curving his lips, "let's."

Drew stared at the photograph on the back of the book jacket. A relaxed, smiling Kathryn Reeves stared back. It was an autographed copy of the book she'd been promoting in San Antonio, inscribed to his mother. He'd bought a copy for himself in San Antonio, along with everything else of hers he could find. And he'd read most of them. They were wonderful stories. Drew knew why she was so popular with her readers. Emotional guts. Kate had them and wasn't afraid to let them show. She reached out and grabbed her audience from the first page.

Reading her had taught him a valuable lesson, one he wasn't ashamed to acknowledge. Good writing was good writing, no matter what the genre.

Funnily enough also, it was through Kate that he'd found an agent. In one of her books, she'd dedicated it to the woman who represented her. It was a simple matter to track the agent down and present his case. Doing so made him feel one step closer to Kate, as if another link had been forged in their bond.

He glanced at his watch. It was late. Most everyone was asleep, having gone to bed hours ago. Unable to relax, he'd gone to the library and scoured the shelves in search of some of the old journals in an attempt to at least do some research and keep his mind focused. It was then that he noticed Kate's books, with Emma's covers. His sister-in-law's artwork lent itself well to Kate's storytelling, complementing the text perfectly. Emma illuminated the words, painting a very real scene, adding to the flavor of the novel, heightening it.

But it wasn't the story that fascinated him right now. It was the woman behind the work. The very real woman he'd made love to in San Antonio.

Memories danced in his head, vividly illustrating the power and beauty of those precious moments. The silky softness of her skin. The pure honesty in her blue eyes when she looked at him. The slight quivering of her flesh when he peeled the thigh-high sheer stockings slowly down each slim leg. The throaty sounds she made as she reached fulfillment. The eagerness to mutually explore the realms of passion.

He'd had no intention of letting her mean more to him than a pleasant, enchanting way to spend the weekend. They were two unencumbered adults. The physical attraction between them had been strong; the strongest he'd ever known. An added bonus, he'd figured. Luck of the draw.

Now he wondered. Was it because in that time that they'd spent with each other, he'd fallen in love, which made the chemistry between them all the more potent?

At first, Drew ignored the telltale signs. He plunged headlong into work, dismissing the fleeting glimpses his mind replayed of Kate at odd times. He pretended that the deep yearnings he experienced were for the wonderful hours they'd shared in that brass bed.

He dated, searching for someone to make him feel the way she had.

It was fruitless. No one did. It wasn't, he realized, the fault of the women he'd seen. They couldn't help the fact that they weren't Kate, could never be Kate. She of the inquisitive mind, the spontaneous laugh, the teasing wit, the genuine warmth, the hidden depths. A woman who was comfortable in her own skin; knew where she was going and where she'd come from. Someone with a unique style and outlook on life. One for whom *hope* and *belief* weren't empty words, but dreams she spun daily.

He fantasized about her. Constantly. Awake or asleep, she was there. He wondered what she was doing, how she'd spent the time apart from him. Was she seeing another man?

That thought rankled. For a man to whom the word

exclusive meant in context to a story, Drew found himself actually thinking of it in terms of a relationship.

He was a man used to coming and going as he pleased; a relationship meant ties, boundaries, commitment. A promise to be there, to consult, to share. All the things he hadn't done before. It implied that you'd gone beyond casual, all the way to involved.

Well, he was involved all right. Heart and body.

Drew quietly closed the book and reshelved it.

Tomorrow morning he would tackle Emma on the subject of Kate, get her advice. Never having been in love before, he wasn't quite sure how to handle wooing a woman in earnest. He had his own ideas, naturally, but were they the right ideas?

So, why not ask a woman, one who knew them both, one he could depend on to be honest.

This love thing, he fancied, was like riding a horse not yet broken—one never knew if he was going to see the ride through smoothly, or if he'd be bucked off, and left to lie in the dust, alone.

It was a little after 9:00 a.m. when Drew went searching for his sister-in-law.

Drew found Emma outside in the studio that Burke had built for her. It was more on the order of a small house, with light streaming into the stone structure from the enormous windows surrounding it. He could see her inside, busily sketching with a pencil, her hand making swift marks on the pad.

He knocked on the etched-glass-and-oak door. "Mind if I come in?"

Emma threw him a welcoming smile and beckoned him inside. "Please do," she called out as he crossed the threshold.

His nephew slept in a nearby cradle, an antique he recognized from its last occupant, Jessie. Drew sauntered over, staring down at the infant.

"Don't wake him," she cautioned. "I just got him back to sleep. That's one hungry baby."

"Samuel's got a Buchanan's appetite, Emma. Larger than life, for everything, or haven't you heard that about us by now?"

She laughed softly. "Oh, I've heard." She rose from her seat on the couch, padding softly in her comfortable, flat ballet-type slippers to the minikitchen. "Care for some coffee?"

He nodded his head, then cautiously moved away from the child. Drew liked this place. It gave one a feeling of peace and space. Sparsely furnished, it was decorated in the Arts and Crafts style of Stickley or Wright. Utilitarian, functional and completely suited to his sister-in-law.

"What are you working on?" he asked as he settled down at the small round table, easing his large frame into the chair.

"I've gotten a commission to do a print for a historical society. Proceeds will be donated for maintaining several historical sites in New Mexico."

"Sometimes I forget that you aren't a native Texan," he said, referring to the fact that before her marriage to Burke, Emma had lived in the neighboring state.

"Don't forget, I still have my house in the mountains. I can't give that place up. I love it up there," she said, a touch of wistfulness in her voice. "Occasionally, Burke and I go there for a weekend." She sipped at her coffee, contained in a generous-size stoneware cup. "But I don't think that you came here to inquire after my house or my future projects." Emma reached out her hand, briefly touching his. "What's up?"

Drew liked her direct manner. "Actually, to be truthful, me."

"How do you mean?"

"I need your advice."

Emma shot him a puzzled glance. "About what?"

A lazy smile kicked up his lips. "Women."

She chuckled. "As if I could tell you something you don't already know. Remember, the Buchanan appetites remark? Well, I've certainly heard about yours with the opposite sex."

"Guilty. I'm not going to deny that I've known my fair share."

"And then some?"

Drew shrugged his shoulders. "Maybe."

"Okay," she said, putting down her cup. "All kidding aside. What is it you want to know?" Emma believed she already had a good idea what he was after.

"Whatever you can tell me about Kate Reeves."

"Kate." Emma considered the inside of her coffee cup for a moment. "Does this have anything to do with what happened between you two in San Antonio?"

His brown eyes were direct. "Did she tell you about it?"

She shook her head. "Nope. Not a word. And," Emma stated, "I never questioned her about the matter, either. Kate's a private person and I thought she might feel uneasy talking about it, as if by doing so I'd wind up being put in the middle if she gave me the details."

Drew hastened to assure Emma, "I don't want you to feel that way."

"What do you want?"

"Her." It was a simple declarative statement that spoke volumes to the right listener.

"Kate's my friend."

"I know. That's why I'm here now."

Emma read the sincerity in his handsome face. "You've given this some thought?"

"I can honestly say that I've thought about little else these past few months." He leaned closer to her. "So much that I can't imagine living the rest of my life without her. Is that honest enough for you?"

Emma sighed, her romantic nature satisfied. "Very." She rested her cheek on her right hand. "I'd guess that you've already got a head start with her just because you've been lovers."

Drew ran one of his hands through his dark brown hair. "Why's that?"

"Because Kate's only had one other serious man in her life, her husband, Jack Terrelli."

Drew put down the cup he'd just raised without taking a drink. "Are you telling me that she's only had one other lover?"

"Is that so surprising?"

"In this day and age, it's practically a miracle."

"There speaks the cynical journalist," Emma observed ruefully. "You'd be surprised, Drew. Not every woman hops in and out of bed. I hadn't. Remember, it's a woman's right to choose, and if she decides to wait, then that's her prerogative also. Just like it was Kate's choice to get involved with you.

"Normally," she admitted, "I wouldn't have divulged that information, but I know it's true, and I think that it might tell you that when she was with you, it wasn't just another roll in the sheets for her. At least, that's my opinion since, as I said, I haven't talked to her about it.'' Emma paused, taking another sip of her coffee. ''And I saw the way she looked at you. As if you were the sun, moon and stars. I saw her look at Jack like that when I met them once in New York.''

Drew replied, ''Exactly like the way you look at Burke.''

''You want my advice, really?'' Emma inquired. ''Just be yourself. Be honest. I do have to warn you, though, it might be an uphill battle. Kate's determined, or at least she was before she met you, to remain unattached. Somehow, I think you may have put a sizable dent in that notion when she was in San Antonio. Work on that.''

He picked up the cup and drank, feeling optimistic about his chances of winning the woman he wanted. ''You approve?''

Emma grinned. ''Why do you think that I invited you to join us that weekend? I thought you two might be right for each other, two people so passionate about their work, their careers, which just happened to involve the same field, writing—and if you didn't hit it off, then no harm was done. I just never expected it to go so far, so fast. Watching you two was like waiting for a storm to hit. There was so much tension in the air, it's a wonder you both didn't set off fires from all the live sparks.'' It was her turn to shrug. ''But that's love. When it hits some people, it hits hard and deep, all the way to the bone and beyond.''

''Yes,'' he echoed quietly. ''Unexpectedly so.''

''Give it your best shot. I'll be rooting for you.''

''Oh, I intend to.'' Drew smiled, a definite kick-ass Texas grin. ''I'm not planning on taking no for an answer.''

Chapter Nine

Kate yawned. She was tired after being up late last night working on the book. She was nearing the end, when the pace generally picked up, which meant she usually worked longer hours in an effort to keep the novel moving toward its conclusion. Trouble was, she'd written and rewritten the last chapter several times.

It was an especially poignant moment in the book; the hero and heroine believed that they had to say goodbye forever. Each time she wrote this love scene, she was reminded of the last hours she'd spent with Drew. Beautiful, wonderful hours lost in the pleasures of his embrace. Searing, tender memories flooded her brain, replaying intimate details over and over again, each one more intense, more erotic than the next.

The brisk bite of the October air hit her face as she took a seat on the wooden swing on the open porch. To combat sitting at her desk most days, Kate took a morning walk after breakfast, and another in the late afternoon, if she could.

This morning she'd needed it to clear her head, so she'd walked and walked, but it wasn't helping. All she could think about was Drew Buchanan. Distance and time certainly hadn't diminished the influence he had over her emotions. It was stronger, sharper. Far from being a chimera, an idle caprice that she'd entered into lightly, her affair weighed heavily on her mind. It stole moments from her work, her social calendar, her every waking hour.

She rocked back and forth. Should she consider getting in touch with him? Would that seem too brazen? Too overtly needy?

Or was she better off not experiencing all the joys to be found with him? Keeping a cool head and a whole heart? Remaining safe in her own world, far away from his?

Drew Buchanan was a threat. To her peace of mind, to her carefully structured life.

Drew Buchanan was a promise. Of delights known; of those that still waited to be explored.

Kate shifted from inward thoughts to those concerns she could handle. Her gaze took in the surrounding area. The garden needed more work. There were hedges to be trimmed. Bushes to be pruned. Maybe even a guest cottage to be added, for visitors who needed their privacy. Her rambling country farmhouse was large, but additional quarters could prove practical. Between her and Jack, they had nieces and nephews, brothers and sisters, cousins—relatives galore. She had friends. A small place for company, for... What? Trysts? Lovers? Like the sweet little house in San Antonio.

Damn! Why did all thoughts eventually lead back to him?

You know why, an inner voice mocked. *You love him.*

Kate couldn't argue with the truth.

A big gray squirrel darted along the oak railing in front of her, a piece of apple in its mouth. He dashed up a nearby evergreen tree, sitting on a low-slung branch, his tiny paws holding the fragment as his teeth made quick work of the slice of fruit.

The squirrel's behavior drew a smile upon her face. Did Drew find enjoyment in the simple everyday life of animals? Would he like to watch the various birds as they came to drink and splash in the birdbaths, or feed in one of the assorted feeders?

There were so many things she didn't know about him. Little details that made life interesting. Questions to fill in the gaps. Like peeling back the layers of one of her characters, discovering what made them tick, she wanted to know more about him. That he was rich, talented, handsome, single, she already knew. She was familiar with the fact that he liked to drive fast cars, listened to vintage rock 'n' roll, that he spoke Spanish with the same agility as English.

But what was his favorite season? Did he like comfort or formality in furniture? She'd never seen his bedroom. Was he a slob? Or fastidious? He'd told her that it was easier for him to use his family's house in San Antonio as a base. Easier? Because he didn't have to set down his own roots?

She liked roots. She liked structure. Having a sense of place, of home, satisfied a deep need in her.

Kate knew he liked good food. But how far did that extend? Was he adventurous there, as well? Had he ever had a sample of her region's cuisine? Had Drew ever tasted sticky buns, or shoofly pie? What about a hoagie or a cheese steak? Creamy rice pudding as only the Amish made it from the local farmers' market.

She could have had the chance to find out some of the answers to her questions—if only she'd taken it. The christening of Samuel Christopher Buchanan would have been the perfect opportunity. Instead, she'd opted out. Gave an excuse that she was already committed to a writers' conference, when in fact, she could have easily changed her mind.

It was the certain knowledge that she would more than likely see Drew again that stopped her from going to Texas. She wasn't ready to face him, or worse yet, have him greet her as just another body in the crowd, a "been there, done that" relationship. Kate didn't think that she could deal well with indifference on his part.

All this, however, was idle speculation on her part.

Kate stood up and called for her dogs, who were running around the front yard, happily playing with a ball. It was time to get back to work. Drew Buchanan could wait.

Drew Buchanan couldn't wait.

He'd hired a car when he arrived at Philadelphia International Airport on the red-eye flight from San Antonio this morning. From Emma, he'd secured Kate's phone number, should he need it. He got her address from a few phone contacts of his own, calling in some favors from friends. It hadn't taken long.

Kathryn Campbell Reeves.

Would she be pleased that he'd decided to pay her a visit?

God, but he hoped so.

Standing there in his room, fresh from the long, hot

shower he'd taken, Drew glanced out the window. The leaves in the various trees were a riot of colors, heralding autumn's robust change.

Change was good. Necessary. It kept one alive, aware, interested.

She lived less than two miles away from the B and B he'd booked into. All he had to do was get dressed, get in the rental car and go there. Show up on her doorstep.

Arrogant.

Yep, he decided, it pretty much was. He didn't expect her to jump into his arms and ravish him on the spot, but he was certainly hoping for a good reaction. This was a courtship, and that had to go slow.

But could he? Having known the refreshing delights to be found with Kate, could he keep the brakes on his emotions, check the rampant desire to bed her as soon as possible?

Drew took the bottle of expensive aftershave and splashed it into his palm, anointing his freshly shaven jaw. Kate had said that she liked the scent. It reminded her of woods and lime. He hoped that it reminded her of him, exclusively.

While he dressed, Drew debated about whether or not to call her and let her know he was here, that he was planning on coming to see her, if she didn't mind.

No. Bad move, he decided. That was the passive way of handling the situation. From experience, he knew one didn't win the tough battles by waiting for permission to proceed. He had to just do it.

As he slipped his wallet into his slacks, Drew thought, what's the worst that she can do? Slam the door in my face? Tell me to get lost? Ask me what the hell I'm doing? Or invite me in. Tell me that she's glad to see me.

If he called her, Kate could hang up. She could pretend to be going out. Having company—or a bad hair day. Be far too busy to have any visitors. Various excuses ran through his mind.

No, showing up would be a fait accompli. He'd be able to gauge her reaction to his spontaneous visit. Her eyes would tell him what he wanted, needed to know. Besides, why had she slept with him if she didn't care in some small way? Emma said that Kate wasn't the offhand type. So that meant that there was a spark to build upon.

He thought about the wrapped presents carefully tucked in his suitcase. Something special for her birthday. A celebration of sorts. He couldn't wait to see the joy on her face when she unwrapped them. Even if they were linked somehow to other memories for her, he'd seen them and knew they were right for Kate.

They'd be for later. Maybe tonight. Maybe tomorrow.

Drew smiled as he slipped into his brown leather jacket. After all, timing, it was said, was everything.

Kate heard the dogs barking excitedly.

Lost in her novel's world of Colonial America, it took a few seconds for her to respond. Hurriedly pushing back her chair, Kate went to the large window that faced the front of her house. An unfamiliar car was coming up the long drive.

She wasn't expecting anyone, and she was set back off the main road so that someone had to make the effort to get to her. She knew the mail woman, who was one of her fans; she joked with the FedEx and UPS deliverymen. But this was no parcel van. It was a small, sporty coupe.

Not waiting to find out who was in the car, she walked out of her room and down the stairs.

The dogs stood at attention at the front door, their fangs bared, growling.

The silhouette of a man was visible through the oval of etched glass.

Her heart skipped a beat. He was very tall.

Could it be?

The doorbell chimed.

Kate licked her suddenly dry lips and softly called off the dogs. "Maverick. Iceman. Heel."

The two collies instantly sat back, silent, watchful as Kate opened the door.

"Drew."

It was said softly, a husky whisper of sound that gladdened his heart. Her wide blue eyes reflected her utter surprise. She had the longest natural lashes of any woman he knew. Brown and thick, they framed those eyes, setting them off. Her hair was only fractionally longer than a few months ago. Still arranged in wild, thick tumbling curls. No lipstick adorned her soft, mobile mouth.

Willpower made Drew stand still instead of sweeping Kate into his arms. God, but she was beautiful. Even more than he remembered, if that were possible.

"Hello, Kate."

Her hand gripped the glass doorknob, unable to let go. She was afraid that her legs might give way, so intense was her reaction to his presence.

"What are you doing here?"

He smiled, the grooves in his cheeks deepening. "Would you believe I was in the neighborhood, just passing through?"

"No, I don't think I would."

"Can I come in? Or would you rather come out?"

"Sorry." She stepped back to allow him entrance. "I seem to have forgotten my manners." Soon, she thought, to be followed by her sanity. Kate couldn't believe this was happening. As if conjured by her own determined mind, Drew was there, standing on her porch, in the flesh. The very desirable flesh.

As he crossed the threshold into her hall, the dogs came instantly alert, growling low in their throats again.

"The faithful Maverick and Iceman, I presume?"

"Yes." Kate knelt and spoke calmly to the dogs. "He's a friend." She turned her head. "Come here and let them get familiar with you."

Drew bent down, holding out both of his hands for the collies to sniff. When that was concluded, he extended them and ruffled each dog's neck, giving both equal attention.

Kate stood up. "It seems as though you've won them over," she observed wryly.

"Part of my Texas charm, sweetheart." He rose, the dogs at his heels. "Remember, I was raised around animals, of all kinds."

Male bonding, Kate thought. Big-time. Instinctively, her dogs trusted him, which impressed her. They generally weren't friendly with strangers.

Kate and Drew stood there, minutes ticking by, each content to simply stare at the other.

"Ah, what are you doing here?" she repeated.

"You didn't believe me when I said that I was passing through?"

Kate smiled, her brows raised skeptically. "Not hardly. Nice try, though."

"I came to see you."

It was the way he emphasized *you* that made her pulse

jump. And those depthless brown eyes. How could she have forgotten the power to be found there? The magnetism? The sheer, sexy animal pull. Looking into his eyes was like diving off a high board—one had to be careful where one landed.

She broke contact for a brief instant. "What for?"

"Do we have to stand here, or can we move somewhere more comfortable?"

"Follow me," she said, leading him down the hallway to the room she used as a living room. It was huge. Bare oak floors gleamed around the edges of a large Chinese wool rug in a soft rose with green accents, complementing the plush sofa and chair upholstered in dark green wool. Small tables flanked either end of the sofa. A low blaze burned behind the glass door of a stone fireplace. Additional wood was stacked neatly in a brass holder.

"Have a seat," she offered. "Can I get you anything?" she said, remembering her social graces. His six-foot-three frame seemed to fill the space.

"Something to drink would be nice," he replied.

"I don't have a ready pitcher of iced tea handy, so will coffee do? Or hot tea?"

"Whatever you're having's fine by me."

"I won't be a minute."

"Take your time. I'm in no hurry." Drew slanted her a glance. "Unless," he inquired, "I've come at a bad time?"

She shook her head. "No. I was just working."

He apologized. "I'm sorry. Have I upset your schedule? I know how I hate being interrupted when I'm in the middle of a story." Concerned, he asked, "Would you like me to come back?"

"That's okay," she replied with a casual wave of her

hand. "I was going to break for lunch soon, anyway. In fact, would you care to stay?"

"Love to."

"Be right back." Kate sailed out of the room, the dogs having opted to stay behind with Drew. She entered her kitchen and put on a fresh pot of coffee, arranging cream and sugar on a decoupage wooden tray she dug up from one of her cabinets.

She watched as the coffee dripped into the machine, arms folded on her chest. He said he'd come here to see her. Why? To pick up where they left off? Or maybe just to say hello, as a friend?

Kate unlinked her arms, moving around the kitchen, anxious.

Talk about an unexpected encounter. It was one thing to muse continuously on one person, as she had on him—then for him to abruptly show up on her doorstep.

She pulled out a seat at the sturdy oak table, plopping down, chin in her palms, her eyes half-closed. He still looked like an ad from a fashion mag. Dressed in olive green corduroy trousers, with an oatmeal-colored sweater under that super leather bomber jacket. Sexy as hell. He looked great in clothes, or out of them.

Her eyes snapped open, looking downward. And here she was, in her baggy, worn sweats.

Oh, well, she rationalized, too damned late now.

Drew removed his jacket, tossing it casually onto the chair. The dogs had settled quietly on the rug, their eyes watchful as he took a few steps toward the other side of the room. He gave a quick glance to the built-in book cabinets that flanked the fireplace. One contained multiple copies of her books, quite a few in foreign editions. He picked one up and flipped through a volume in Chinese. On the other side were well-read copies of several other well-known romance writers.

He turned his head and noticed the silver-framed photos on one of the end tables. He'd seen a few pictures hanging in the hallway when he'd come in. Walking back over, Drew examined them more closely. There was one of Kate with an older couple, all smiles. Probably her parents. Another, obviously taken when she was younger, maybe while in high school, with a young man and two women. There was a resemblance between them, so he assumed it was Kate with her siblings.

One photograph in particular stood out to Drew. It was of a man. The photographer had captured the hint of laughter in the eyes, the relaxed mood of the subject. Unlike the others, it wasn't in color. Black and white suited the handsome man better. It was moody, classic.

"That was my husband."

Drew looked in the direction of the doorway. Kate stood there, a tray in her hands.

He put the framed shot back down on the table. "That was a happy man, someone who loved life."

She smiled bittersweetly. "Yes, on both counts." Kate set the tray down on the low coffee table, taking a seat on the couch. Drew joined her. His nearness brought every atom in her body screaming to life. Would his kiss be as wonderful as she remembered it?

"Why are you here?" she asked again as she handed him his coffee.

"Like I said, to see you." He examined the image on the tray. Ripe bunches of red, white and purple grapes hung heavily on vines, ready to be harvested. They looked so real, as if they could be lifted from off the tray and into his hands.

Kate leaned back, crossing one leg over the other, sipped at her coffee. "Really?"

"You sound as if you don't believe me?"

"I can't think of a reason for the visit."

"Oh, can't you?" he asked, his voice low and tender.

The walls of the room felt as if they were closing in on her. Her breathing deepened. It wouldn't do any good to pretend. It must have something to do with their affair.

A sudden horrible thought struck her. Was he ill? Oh God, no, she prayed silently. Not this handsome, vital man. Oh, please, no, not him.

Drew saw the change in Kate's features. Her eyes widened, her hand flew to her mouth.

"What's wrong?"

She swallowed nervously. "It's not about your health, is it?"

The truth of the matter dawned on him. "No, you can relax. I'm perfectly healthy. *Very* healthy," he stressed. "And planning on remaining so for a long time."

She expelled a deep breath. "That's a relief."

Her concern had been, he could tell, for him. Her guard had been let down. She did care. At least a little. "Sorry if I led you to think otherwise." Drew put his cup down and reached out his hand, taking hers. "I came here to see you. To spend some time with you, if you'll allow me."

"What?"

"You heard me," he said in that sexy Texas drawl. "I want to be with you. Was I wrong in thinking that you'd like to be with me?"

Kate wet her lips, setting her cup down with her free hand. She hadn't expected this. It was all so sudden.

"Time passed," he explained. "I found that I couldn't forget you. What we shared that weekend was special—

I'd like to think to both of us. Something that doesn't come along every day.''

He was speaking the words she'd wanted to hear; yet, conversely, she was afraid to hear. ''So, what you're saying is that you'd like to resume our...'' the word *affaire* stuck in her throat, even if it was the correct term to use. Emotionally, she was still trying to process the content of his words.

''Relationship,'' he put in.

''For how long?''

Drew wanted to say ''forever,'' but gambled that now wasn't the right time. It might scare her as much as it had scared him. It had only come lately to him that he wanted this thing between them to continue, to grow. But what if she didn't feel the same? ''As long as it takes.''

''For what?''

''To burn itself out or go on.'' Drew waited for her to respond. ''Talk to me, Kate.''

''San Antonio was wonderful,'' she began, wondering how to put her jumbled feelings into words. It should be easy for her, she was a writer. But it wasn't. Truth be told, it was a struggle to determine how to answer him. One part of her yearned to say, let's go for it. The other urged caution. God knows it wasn't a question of want. She wanted him now, more than ever. ''But,'' she said, trying to clarify the situation, ''it was an incident that had a defined lifetime, a set end.''

''Was it really over for you?'' He leaned closer. ''Tell me you haven't thought about it since then, or about us. Tell me you haven't lain awake nights remembering the passion we experienced, the genuine heat between us.'' His hand touched her shoulder, slipping upward under the fall of her hair, caressing her neck, her earlobe. "Tell me."

"I can't," she whispered.

"I thought so. You haven't forgotten. You *couldn't* forget or ignore something so powerful, so fiery. It doesn't come along all that often. I ought to know."

"What makes you so sure that what we shared is different?" It had been for her. She knew that already.

"I just am."

Kate looked into his eyes. She voluntarily reached out her hand and brushed a thick lock of almost-black hair back off his forehead. In that moment, she saw traces of the boy he must have been: brash, confident, charming and, above all, honest. It was all there in the man before her.

"So, what do you propose?"

He'd clearly scored some major points with her. "That we get to know each other better."

Kate almost laughed at the thought. They'd been as intimate as two people could be, but she understood what he was saying. "I can't put my life on hold for you, Drew, nor would I expect you to put yours in limbo for me."

"I'm not asking you to. I'll make do with your schedule."

"And what about yours?"

"Let's say that time isn't important to me right now. I'm keeping a low profile."

That made her laugh. "You?" she asked, skepticism evident in her tone.

He grinned. "Oh, I've got a few irons in the fire, but nothing I can talk about at present."

Secrets.

He saw the slightly hurt look in her eyes. "Trust me. I'll tell you when the time is right."

"When will that be?" Why couldn't he tell her now? Was he working on something dangerous again?

"Soon, I hope."

This was crazy, she thought. He wanted to renew their affaire, for who knew how long. Just pick up and proceed. See where it went.

Could she? Should she? With no guarantees?

Didn't she owe it to herself?

But what about the hurt she was leaving herself open for? She'd walked away from him once. Could she do it again should things fall apart? It was such a risk.

He wanted a trial. It was easy to be analytical when he was a thousand miles away from her, when she didn't have to see his face inches from hers, or feel the warmth of his skin. Sitting here, so close to her, it was much harder for Kate to be objective.

Drew watched her face. It was another thing he liked about Kate—her features were open, as opposed to robotically perfect, or ice-cold. He could tell she was struggling. He could empathize with that, for he was, too.

"All right." The words slipped out of her mouth.

Drew relaxed. "Good. What about dinner tonight? Are you free?"

Breaking the tension, Kate used an old comic line, her quirky sense of humor coming to the fore. "No, but I'm reasonable."

Drew chuckled.

This time she answered him honestly. "I'd love to have dinner with you."

"Then you pick a place."

"Why not here?"

"You'll cook?"

"I may not be Julia Child, but I can cook."

"Then I'd be pleased."

"Come by around seven, then."

"I should let you get back to work if I'm going to tie up your evening."

"You've changed your mind, you won't stay for lunch?"

"No." Going slow was going to be tough. "I've got some work I can do, as well."

"Where are you staying?"

Drew mentioned the name of the bed-and-breakfast and Kate recognized it as a rather well-known one in Chester County. "Yes, I know of The Hunt Lodge. Quite a good reputation."

"I'll bring the wine."

"No need," she assured him. "I've got some on hand that I think will do nicely."

"Then—" he stood up, retrieving his jacket and bidding his farewell to the collies "—till tonight."

Kate walked him to the front door and followed him onto the porch. He turned and dropped a quick, light kiss on her mouth before striding down the stone steps. A ghost of a smile played on her face as she watched him get into his rented car and drive away.

What had she let herself in for?

Chapter Ten

Kate went through her large walk-in closet, desperately looking for something to wear.

She wasn't exactly sure what mood to project tonight. Casual. Upscale. Formal. Sexy. What? her mind questioned.

She rejected formal outright. Cooking dinner in a linen suit wasn't her idea of a good time. Besides, this wasn't a business meeting. Far from it.

Perhaps something soft, that said she was approachable. Something sexy, showing off her shapely figure, to make him notice—or better yet, remember.

Maybe her favorite well-washed jeans and a sweater. Something that told him he was welcome.

No. Tonight needed a special touch.

Kate gave a quick glance at her watch. Drew would be here within the hour.

What she needed was an outfit that said smart, sophisticated, sensual, with an added touch of sassiness. Kate pulled a few items from her capacious closet, matching and mixing colors until she found exactly what she wanted. She'd save the one dress she'd debated about wearing tonight for another occasion. There was bound to be a more formal setting for one of their evenings, or at least she hoped there would be. Tonight, Kate wanted Drew to feel at ease in her home. To see another side of her.

As she walked out of the closet, she gave a lingering glance at her bed, to the wideness of the queen-sized frame. It had been bought for style and comfort, a bed only she'd slept in. She'd given the one she'd slept in with Jack to his younger sister and her husband since it was a Terrelli family piece. After he'd died, Kate couldn't bear to sleep in that bed again, alone; the memories were too painful.

What, she wondered, would Drew look like there in hers? It was a cherry sleigh bed, covered with plump cream pillows of all shapes and sizes, a down-filled comforter in brown and cream.

And how would she feel if he did share it with her, then left? As empty as she had felt before with the loss of Jack? Could she still look at it as hers and hers alone then? Or would her Texan imprint himself on this room, on her furniture, as he had done on her?

Kate smiled at the words: her Texan.

Was he really? And if so, for how long?

Perhaps the better question to ask was how long did she want?

Kate couldn't come up with an answer. At this point in time, she truly didn't know. Until forever? Until next week? The week after that? Till Christmas? The New

Year? Until her heart broke yet again? She just wasn't sure.

She moved away, unwrapping the towel from around her just-washed hair. Its natural curl sprang to life, so that all she had to do was rub the towel over it a few times to remove any traces of dampness. Her bureau held several bottles of perfume. She cocked her head, looking at the fragrances. A smile came over Kate's lips as her left hand reached out and selected one, a gardenia scent, the same one that she'd been wearing in San Antonio. She applied it to her throat, to the fold of her arm, her wrists. Would he remember?

Putting the glass stopper back in the bottle, her eyes focused on her wedding ring. She wore it proudly, with deep love for the man who'd put it there. Her right hand covered it, fingertips sliding over the gold band. Kate lifted her head, her eyes meeting those of her reflected self in the mirror. It had been a part of her life for so long.

Kate glanced back down. The past was gone. Nothing she could do would ever bring it back. Wasn't tonight about discovering whether or not there was a future with someone else? About moving on?

She twisted the ring off her finger, her hand looking suddenly naked. Kate grasped the ring in her palm, holding on to it tightly for a moment before bringing it to her lips, her fingers unclenched. With her left hand, she flipped open the lid on one of her jewelry boxes, and, kissing the gold band, she placed the ring in a compartment and put it away.

It was time to let go.

Kate took a deep, intense breath. She had to get ready. Drew would be here before she knew it, and she wanted to get dinner started so that they could relax, or at least attempt to.

Was he feeling as excited as she?

He was.

Drew wanted everything to be perfect, or as close to it as he could possibly make it. After all, he'd never been in love before. Long term wasn't part of his modus vivendi.

Kate had changed all that. Powerfully. Passionately. Unquestionably. She was the catalyst, much as Emma had been for Burke. It was Kate's fault if he'd started to believe in happily-ever-after, in the reality of dreams. His no-nonsense approach to life had irretrievably altered. All because of one weekend; one woman.

Drew tapped out a message on the keyboard of his laptop, pressing the send command. *So far, so good.*

Almost immediately there was a response. *Congratulations!*

Drew grinned. *Not yet,* he wrote.

I have faith in you, big brother. Nothing's ever stopped you before from going after what you want— and getting it.

There's always a first time, Drew answered.

I don't think that Kate is going to be the exception.

I'm certainly gonna do my damnedest to make sure she isn't!

Spoken, or in this instance, written like a true Buchanan, Burke acknowledged.

Thanks, Burke. I'm glad that you're in my corner, little brother.

Always.

Drew added a few personal remarks and ended the

connection. He pushed back the sleeve of his burgundy sweater, checking the time on his Rolex.

Kate was expecting him.

For a wealthy man, Drew was as much at ease in her kitchen as he was in a four-star restaurant. It was one of the things Kate loved about him. He had money, class and breeding, plus the guts to make it on his own in a very competitive field. He didn't hide behind a wall of servants, or play at working, or amuse himself with idle pursuits. He was, she was finding out, unlike anyone she'd ever known.

"So, you like the idea of speed, of going faster than a Texas twister?" he asked, sipping his glass of chilled sparkling wine.

"I can't explain it," Kate responded, stirring the contents of the nonstick frying pan with a wooden spoon, adding a dash of salt and pepper. "I really like flying. Taking off in a jet plane is such a rush. I love it. But, to be in a jet, actually at the controls, well," she said, her tone wistful, "that would be fantastic." Kate lifted the lid on another pot, stirring the ingredients there, as well. "It's probably one of the main reasons—not to mention all the hunky-looking men—why I loved *Top Gun*. Watching all those fighter pilots taking off in their supersonic jets from the deck of the carrier. I confessed to major pilot envy right then, wishing I was there, inside one of them, if only for a moment."

"Have you ever taken a lesson?"

"Me?" Kate shook her head. "Nope. Don't have the time."

"Bull."

She turned around to face him, arms akimbo. "Say what?"

"You heard me, sweetheart. If you wanted to, you could easily find the time."

Kate picked up her glass, sampling some of the wine. "You're right, I could," she acknowledged. "Maybe later."

"I've done it."

"Done what?"

"Flown in a fighter jet."

Kate's blue eyes widened. "You have? When?"

"Three years ago. I was doing a story on some good ole Texas boys, fighter pilots, and since one of them was a cousin of my college roommate, I had a chance to find out what it's like. The fact that I also have a pilot's license didn't hurt, either."

"You fly?"

Drew smiled. "I've been known to on occasion."

"Why?" She imagined she already knew the answer. It was a challenge—and it was dangerous.

"Because I wanted to. We've had planes at the ranch since before I was born. I just sort of picked it up, then decided it might be fun to take it one step further." He moved across the room. "I could take you up sometime if you'd like."

"Perhaps."

Drew stood next to her, looking down. "Don't trust me?"

"It's not that," Kate said, tilting her head back.

"Then," he said in that sexy, dark as malt voice, "what is it?"

She wanted to say, don't promise something you may not be around to do. Plans change; people change; things happen.

Drew lifted her chin with his hand. "Talk to me."

"I don't want to talk about the future, about maybes

or promises. Let's just take it as it comes, okay?'' she asked. "No pledges, no obligations.''

"If that's what you want. Keep in mind, the offer's always open.''

"I will." She reached her hand up, softly touching his face with a gliding stroke before gently pushing at the stray lock of hair that had fallen on his forehead. "I'm glad you're here.''

"Are you?''

"Don't," she insisted, "doubt it." Kate slid her hand around his neck and pulled his head down to hers, brushing her lips across in the lightest of caresses.

"Dinner's almost ready," she said, breaking contact, "so why don't you take a seat and let me get it.''

Bemused by her actions, Drew complied. He watched as she moved economically around the space, fixing a plate for each of them. He found he liked watching her, even doing ordinary things like spooning rice onto a china plate, followed by the chicken and diced tomatoes recipe. She was wearing an off-the-wall apron, advertising a cookbook, a souvenir she'd told him, from a recent booksellers' trade show promo. It was totally incongruous with what lay underneath.

How could anyone look so damned sexy in such tame clothes? he marveled. Basic classic style, from the cashmere turtleneck sweater in deep brown, belted into a pair of cream wool cuffed trousers. Sensible flat brown leather shoes and trouser socks completed the outfit. Perfectly respectable. Perfectly composed.

So why was his temperature soaring? Because he knew what lay below the surface of the materials that covered her from head to toe?

Probably. But it was more than that. Much more. It

was the confidence Kate exuded. Like an aura, it surrounded her.

Drew had also taken sharp note of what she wasn't wearing tonight. Her wedding ring was missing. That, he concluded, was a good sign, indicative of progress. Another man's ring was another man's claim.

One less reminder of the past was a point in his favor.

Having finished the delicious meal that Kate prepared, they settled in for dessert. She'd promised him a surprise, something very Philadelphian.

A fire blazed in the hearth, the heat keeping the kitchen toasty warm. It also gave a heightened sense of intimacy to the experience of dining alone together, as if they were already a solidly established couple. Through the various windows, star-spangled darkness surrounded them. They were alone, save for the two collies, enclosed in a world of their own. No streetlamps, no outside noises, no distractions of any kind. Just two people content with each other's company.

"You don't mind being this isolated?" Drew inquired as Kate slipped the dirty dishes into the dishwasher.

"That's one of the reasons I love it so much," she explained, stacking the utensils in their plastic bin. "After living in the city for so long, it was great to find a spot where intrusions aren't commonplace. Fire engines, police sirens, ambulances, billboards, the general sounds of urban landscape. They were the norm in Philly. A constant barrage of the senses. I made do because Jack had to live there.

"Don't get me wrong, I love Philly. But I can't live there, or in any city, anymore. It's just not where I feel the most comfortable. I like going into town as a change of pace. And," she smiled, facing him, "New York's a kick anytime. Occasionally I go and stay there for a few days, see my agent and editor, then do whatever I feel like: shop, see some shows, go to a few new restaurants, visit a museum." She closed the door of the dishwasher with a firm snap. "Knowing that this is waiting here for me makes every trip away all that more worthwhile." Her face glowed. "This house is my sanctuary. My roots, as it were."

Kate pulled out a filter from the box and scooped coffee into it, sliding it into the machine and setting the coffee on to brew. "Have you ever felt that way about a place?" she asked.

"Can't say as I have," Drew admitted, qualifying his response with, "at least not as strongly as you. Guess that I've been too much of a rolling stone." He grinned. "Of course, it goes without saying that I love Texas."

Kate cut in, "As if I couldn't tell that. I've yet to meet anyone from that state who doesn't. You're like all the rest, a Texan first and foremost."

"Just about."

"A breed apart from other states, other men," she commented.

Drew shrugged his wide shoulders. "Well, I don't know about that."

"Oh, but you are," Kate insisted. "There's a certain arrogance, a bigger-than-life quality about a lot of you, an innate sense of superiority."

"You make us sound conceited and smug."

Kate laughed. "Aren't you?"

Drew returned her smile. "Remember what that woman told us when we stopped for gas? 'Texans are the best, and then there's the rest.'"

"Enough said."

He raised one thick, dark brow. "I think that there's a compliment in there somewhere."

Kate lifted two large coffee-bar-size cups from the overhead cabinet. "You could be right."

"And I suspect," he observed, "a sneaking admiration from a certain Yankee lady. So why haven't you set a book in Texas yet?"

"How do you know I haven't?"

"Because I recall you telling Emma that you were thinking about it, and," he said, looking her straight in the eyes, "I've read your books."

"You have?" Kate was wildly pleased and patently surprised. "Which one?"

"When I said I read them, I meant I read them *all*, Kate."

"All?"

"Yes," he reiterated. "I thought that I'd try just one, to sample it after having met you. See what it was like. How you wrote."

"And?"

"I found I liked it."

"Which surprised you, didn't it?"

Drew grinned.

"You're not the first person to tell me that," she stated. "I've heard that sentiment expressed before. So many people put down romance novels without even trying one of them. Then, when they do, they're more often than not amazed that they enjoyed the book." Kate stepped closer to him, her hand reaching out and grasping his forearm; she could feel the strong muscles beneath the layer of his sweater. "I'm glad that you liked my work."

"It wasn't hard to like, sweetheart," he readily admitted. "You're good. In fact, damn good. With each book I picked up, you got me hooked from the very first page, so it was no hardship, I can tell you, to keep on reading.'' Drew slipped his hand over hers, squeezing it lightly. "So, what are you working on now?"

With that question Kate pulled away from his grasp, turning back to the kitchen counter. She wet her lips. "Colonial America," she said, her tone husky.

"Sounds interesting."

"It is, very," she said, cutting open the string that held the lid closed on the boxed item she'd bought earlier for dessert.

"What's it about?"

"Five hundred pages or so." She looked over her shoulder at his face, needing some humor to lighten up the situation. "Sorry. I couldn't resist. A sort of in-joke among some writer friends of mine. It's about people caught up in the American Revolution in Virginia."

"Could I sneak a peak?"

"I'm afraid not," she said. "I don't like anyone to see what I'm writing until I'm done."

"I can respect that, so when will that be?"

"Soon, I hope. It's not due for another two months, but I seem to have been lucky with this book. It's going quite well, quicker than some of my others, at least in spots."

"Only in spots?"

"Yeah. Some days it's easy, others, like pushing a rock up a mountain." *Especially,* she thought, *since the hero looks exactly like you.*

Kate cut apart several pieces of the dessert, arranging them on a large plate. "What about you? Does your own writing come fast?"

"Most times."

"And your new project?"

"If it gets approval, I'll be involved with it for quite a while. Maybe a year or more."

Was this a hint that this interlude might only be, in fact, temporary? "In or out of the country?"

"In. And that's all I'm going to say right now."

Kate threw him a curious glance. "You're being awfully mysterious." Probably because it was dangerous, she thought. If it were routine profiles, he'd have surely told her, hinted at the truth, at least. Since he hadn't, it must be something hot. An investigation of homegrown terrorists, gunrunners or maybe hate groups. Kate swallowed the fear that rose in her throat, keeping it bottled inside.

"I have a confession to make," she said as she put small plates, along with fresh cutlery and napkins on the table. "I've read some of your work, as well."

It was Drew's turn to be surprised. "How did you get ahold of it?"

"Easy," she explained. "Via the Internet. I located *Lone Star Monthly*'s web site, logged on and pulled up some of your pieces, then downloaded them to read later." Her words were honest. "You're good, too. You paint very strong word pictures, Drew. Vivid. You don't pull punches, but you're not cruel or petty."

"Why, thank you, ma'am," he drawled. "Kidding aside, that means a lot to me coming from you, sweetheart." Drew watched as she placed the dessert on the table. "Now, what have we here?"

"Sticky buns."

"One of your area specialities, right?"

"You betcha." Kate poured their coffee. "I defy you to eat just one," she declared. "These are delicious. So rich, you won't believe. I don't allow myself these but twice a year. Just looking at them adds ten pounds, I swear."

"That shouldn't matter to you." Drew gave Kate's trim, curvy figure a long and lingering glance.

"Liar."

"Oh, no, darlin'," he protested, "it's the truth."

"Bless you." Kate ignored her small fork and picked up the bun, unwrapping the flaky layers with her fingers, tearing off a piece at a time. The sticky glaze coated her fingers, and when she went to lick it off, Drew's deep baritone stopped her.

"Let me," he said, taking her hand in his, bringing it to his lips. His tongue made a slow pass up each digit, before his mouth captured and sucked each finger clean of the syrupy coating. "Sweet," he murmured.

Kate's insides quivered.

"You're right," he said when he successfully completed his task, releasing her hand. "This is a great dessert." Drew abandoned his fork and followed her example.

"My turn." Kate mimicked his actions completely. She could tell the effect it was having upon Drew by the increased snap of his pulse under her fingertips as she held his wrist secure. His eyes were intense, smoldering, so warm she could feel the heat beneath her clothes.

She was so tempted to forget decorum and beg him to take her there, right in the kitchen. Make love to her on the floor. The table. The counter. Wherever he wanted so long as he didn't let her go.

But she wouldn't. They'd already had fast and furious. Now it was time for slow and sure. Time to see if there was something else.

Drew cleared his throat, breaking the spell. "We could do this all night, but I don't think we should." He recognized the pitfalls of continuing on.

Kate sighed. "You're probably right."

Minutes ticked by as they ate their dessert in companionable silence, stealing glances at each other.

"Would you like another?" Kate asked, rising from her chair, pouring another cup of coffee for them both.

"I'll pass," Drew answered.

Kate added cream to her cup, dusting the top with a sprinkle of chocolate. "I meant to ask you, how did you find me?"

His smile was enigmatic. "I had my ways."

"Such as?" She wondered if his sister-in-law helped him. "Emma?"

"She gave me your phone number after I explained the situation."

Kate's eyes were sharp. "What did you say?"

"Not very much, actually. She knew about us."

Kate nodded. "I figured she might. Emma's very perceptive." She sipped at the hot liquid. "I didn't mention anything to her for fear of putting her in the middle, which wouldn't have been fair."

"She thought that's how you'd feel," he said. "All I asked her for was your phone number, since I tried and found it unlisted. Getting your address was a matter of knowing some people and getting them to do me a favor."

"Money talks, eh?"

"It helps in some instances," he admitted ruefully, "but in this case, it was payback time for past good turns."

She gave him a grateful smile. "Well, I'm glad that whatever it took, you came."

"So am I." Drew glanced at the clock on the wall. "I suppose I should be getting back."

"Do you have to?"

He was pleased to hear the disappointment in her

voice. "Yes." If he didn't, Drew realized that he'd break his resolve and take her now, so strong was the temptation. He wanted to be with her, watch her, listen to her. He ached with that need.

Kate didn't want him to go. It felt so right having him there, in her kitchen, sharing a meal, sharing time. So right that she didn't want to question for how long, and if she could handle it for the long term. All she knew was that she was in danger of falling deeper in love with Drew Buchanan every minute that passed.

"Let me get your coat, then."

Drew followed Kate down the hallway, stopping her before she could retrieve his leather jacket from the hall tree. He slipped his arms around her waist and drew her into his kiss.

At first it was soft, full of promise. Then it changed, growing harder, deeper, more intimate in every way.

Kate burrowed closer to his strength, leaning into his warmth, her hands anchoring themselves in his sweater, pulling him to her.

Drew backed her up to the wall, one hand tangled in her hair, the other sliding around to cup her breast. The feel of the cashmere under his palm, the push of her nipple against the barriers that separated it from him, fueled his fire. Each caress only intensified his hunger. Made him long for more.

The barking of the two dogs abruptly broke the mood.

Suddenly, Drew pulled back, breaking off contact with Kate. He took in several deep gulps of air, trying to calm his racing heart. He watched as Kate's eyes opened, staring at him.

When she spoke, her voice was husky. "That was some good-night kiss."

Drew brushed his thumb across the slightly swollen pout of her lips. "One of the best."

A glimmer of a smile crossed Kate's mouth. "Only *one* of the best?"

Drew smiled also. "Okay. *The* best. Happy?"

"Actually, very."

"Good." He shot a look at the now silent dogs, who watched the couple, their tails wagging, tongues lolling.

"They're not used to this," she offered by way of explanation.

Drew turned and addressed the dogs, circling one arm about Kate's waist. "Better *get* used to this, boys. You'll be seeing a whole lot more of it."

"Will they?" she asked softly.

Drew angled his head, looking down at Kate's up-turned face. "Count on it, sweetheart. When a Texan stakes a claim, he doesn't allow anything or anyone to interfere, man nor beast."

"And is that what you're doing? Staking a claim?"

"Don't you ever doubt it." Drew lifted her chin and kissed her quickly. "I'll call you first thing in the morning."

"No," she replied, walking with him to the front door, flipping the switch that flooded the porch with light. "Call me when you get back to your room. I don't want to wait until morning."

They stood outside, each finding it hard to let the other go.

"Get back inside," he urged. "It's too cold out here for you."

"Wuss," she teased. "It's nothing."

"I can see you're cold." He slipped his hands inside his jacket pockets to pull out his gloves, and found the gifts he'd stashed there for her birthday. "Damn, I almost forgot. I brought these for you, for your special day tomorrow.''

''You remembered?'' Kate accepted the packages, her expression alight with pleasure. ''Shall I open them now?''

''Why don't you wait till tomorrow? It'll give me an excuse to come back so that I can see your face.''

''You don't need an excuse, Drew.'' Kate's eyes sparkled, and like a child, she shook the elegantly wrapped boxes. ''But if you insist, then come for breakfast.''

''If you want.''

Want. More than you can ever imagine, darling.

''I do.''

''Then breakfast it will be.'' He stroked her cheek with one finger. ''Good night.''

''Happy trails, Tex,'' she whispered as he walked down the steps and across the lawn in the direction of his rental car.

Kate dashed back inside the warm comfort of her home, watching from her doorway as his car sped off into the night. Happiness bubbled up inside her.

Could she believe in love enough to give it a second chance—could she take the ultimate gamble again?

Or did she only want to keep it a game, without raising the stakes?

Kate thought about the gifts, the evening that they'd spent together. He was making it difficult to choose.

Chapter Eleven

Early the next morning, Kate walked through the open doors to her office, a large cup of coffee in her hand. She was in a wonderful mood, light and cheery. In another hour or so, she'd be with Drew.

Last night, when Drew reached the inn where he was staying, he'd kept his word and called her. They'd spent almost an hour on the phone, talking, laughing, making plans for the day, each reluctant to break the connection. They'd both been in bed, which made the conversation seem somehow more intimate, more elemental. Tucked up beneath a comforter, pillows piled behind her, Kate was relaxed and responsive.

Today, they were going for a scenic drive, allowing her the opportunity to play tour guide for him. Kate wanted to show him a bit of her area, give Drew a feel for where she lived, show him the glorious beauty of her favorite season, as many of the trees still had vibrant color.

Later, Drew wanted to take her out for dinner, to celebrate her birthday in style. She'd agreed, and when she said that she'd make reservations, he told her to forget it; he'd already taken care of it.

"Where are we going?"

"It's a surprise," he'd responded.

"Well," she demurred, "I would like to know how I should dress. Are we talking burger joint or something a bit more upscale?"

He laughed. "Definitely big-time, sweetheart. Trust me, you won't regret one minute, I promise you."

How could she, if the time was spent with him?

But before that, or the rest of the day, Kate had to take care of answering some mail. Fan letters had been accumulating; she whittled the pile down until only a few remained. If she was lucky, she might be able to get off two or more before he showed up.

Turning on her laptop, she saw the indication that she had some electronic mail waiting, as well. Kate wondered if there would be another message from the person who identified himself, or herself, only by the moniker of Wizard. Whoever it was, the person had left a variety of random greetings for her. When she'd tried to find out who it was, the on-line profile was blank. Obviously, the sender didn't want anyone to know his or her real identity.

Kate retrieved her message and found that, sure enough, there was one more from Wizard. She hit the print button, adding the piece of paper to her collection, trying to figure out what the meaning behind the notes was.

She read them all.

*"No Spring, nor Summer beauty hath such grace,
As I have seen in one Autumnal face."*

What did they all mean? They were lines from a poem, that much she'd grasped. But what did they have to do with her?

Perhaps she should show them to Drew? He might have a take on what they could be.

Or would he think her silly? No harm was being done. They weren't threatening. Still, it was a puzzle.

"So, what do you think?"

"Harmless," Drew pronounced.

"Really?"

"He…"

Kate cut in. "You think it's a man?"

Drew scanned the printed sheets. "More than likely."

"A fan?"

"Could be. How long has this been going on?"

"Less than two weeks," Kate answered. "And I can't trace him."

"Is this upsetting you?" He stood beside her as she broke eggs into a bowl and whipped them into a frothy batter.

Kate read the concern for her in his eyes. "Not distressing me so much as piquing my curiosity."

Drew grinned. "A rival? Should I worry?"

"Not hardly," she replied. "I have a feeling that there's a clue in there somewhere, but I must be missing it." Kate shrugged her shoulders. "Okay. Let's not waste any more time on it. I'd rather have breakfast and open my presents, anyway."

Within minutes, Kate served up thick French toast,

adding a sprinkle of cinnamon to each slice. Warm maple syrup was drizzled over it all.

"You're a great cook, you know that?" Drew asked, refilling his cup.

Kate beamed. "Thanks. I like cooking, even if I don't get to do it all that often."

"Why not?"

"I don't care to go to all that trouble for just myself," she admitted. "Maybe once a week or so I'll fix up some stuff that I can freeze and thaw out later. Most of the time, though, I fix something light and quick. It's easier that way."

"I know. Eating alone isn't great."

"Can you cook?"

"Oh, I can rustle up a few basic things," he acknowledged, "nothing fancy though. Just grub. Mostly steak, and I can microwave a mean baked potato. Luckily, if I'm at home in San Antonio, Selena cooks. If not, and I'm on assignment, there are usually always restaurants within reach and hotel fare." He sat down again. "Did you cook for Jack?"

Kate found it was becoming easier to talk to Drew about her late husband. "Sometimes. We traded off most days. He was a good cook, mainly Italian dishes that he learned from his *nonna*," she said. "Grandmother Terrelli was a wonder in the kitchen—still is. Her lasagna was to die for. As was Jack's mother's Irish stew and soda bread. She always has that for me when I stop by."

With his napkin, he wiped away a trace of maple syrup from his lips. "Do you keep in close touch with your in-laws?"

"I don't see them as often as I'd like, but I try and give Jack's folks a call every couple of weeks to say hello and see how they're doing. I have dinner with his sister once a month or so, depending on our schedules.''

''What about your own parents?''

A sunny smile lit up Kate's face. ''They live down the shore. Avalon. Right on the beach. It's marvelous.''

''You like the ocean?''

''God, yes,'' she said enthusiastically, ''I love it. Especially now, in autumn. It's fun to walk along the beach when it's colder. Without the crowds, without the heat. Just the sand, the water and the waves. And of course, the seagulls. Can't forget them.''

''I'd like to meet your parents,'' Drew announced.

''Would you?'' Kate finished the last bit of her French toast, wiping the piece around the plate, sopping up the remains of the syrup.

''Sure. That is, if you don't mind?'' He wanted to know more about her, where she came from, what her family was like. It was a continual surprise to him that no detail was too boring or insignificant for him to discover. Before, background had been for articles, not for people. With Kate, his interest ran deep and wide.

Mind? Kate thought. She'd love to introduce Drew to her folks. But as what? Her lover? As a potential mate? As the man she was head over heels in love with?

Safer to say he was a friend. A *good* friend. A *close* friend.

''I'd like that,'' she answered.

''So would I.''

''Then, I'll give them a call and see if it's all right with them if we come down.''

Kate got up and reached for the extension that was in the kitchen, pushing the speed-dial button for her parents.

Drew watched her, his eyes slowly traveling along the

pathway from the crown of her head down the sleek line of her back, covered by a white oxford shirt and navy blue vest, to the soft curve of her bottom, outlined by a pair of snug jeans, to the length of her legs. He wanted to slide his hands up and down every inch of her, with and without clothes. Cupping, hugging, squeezing, touching, worshiping every centimeter of her shapely body.

His own jeans felt tighter as his body reacted instantly to his erotic thoughts, the fabric straining against the rise of his manhood beneath it. Kate was a human spark to his libido, sending it flaring to life. Brighter. Deeper. Stronger. Faster. Sweeter. Fiercer. Like no other woman, she alone fanned the flames of passion into love.

He wanted to introduce her to his own parents, Noah and Santina Buchanan. They'd adore her, he was sure. What, he reckoned, wasn't to like about Kate? Bright and beautiful, successful in her own right, not overly impressed with the Buchanan fortune and position, with a deeply loving heart.

He could almost laugh at his former arrogance regarding love.

"Can't say as I feel any older, Mom." Kate stretched the cord of her phone as she sat down, one hand sliding across the table to link with Drew's. She laughed. "I'm going out tonight. Uh-huh. A birthday dinner." She sliced Drew a pointed glance. "Well, sort of," she said. "It's a long story, Mom, one I'll tell you more about later, Okay? Yes, he is sitting right across from me. We're spending the day together.

"Describe him? Hmm." Kate gave the man she loved a long, assessing look. "I hate to admit that I can't quite top that old stereotypical phrase—tall, dark and handsome.'' She grinned at the pleased face Drew wore at hearing her comments.

''Respectable?'' Kate smiled. ''He comes from a very good family. No, I don't think you know them. Out of state.''

Drew picked up her hand and turned it over, his lips caressing her open palm.

Kate's pulse rate increased; she pulled her hand away. ''Would you mind if I brought my friend—'' she watched as Drew mouthed the last word to her with a raised brow ''—down for the weekend? You wouldn't? Great.''

Color flooded Kate's cheeks. ''No, two bedrooms will be fine. Is daddy there? No, don't bother him, then. Okay. Love you.'' Kate hung up the phone.

''It's all set. They'll be expecting us tomorrow.''

Drew lifted his hand and stroked his index finger across the pink-tinged skin of her cheekbone, which only made Kate blush deeper. ''Sweet,'' he murmured.

She shrugged. ''Guess I'm not quite as nonchalant about bringing you to meet my folks.''

''I think that it was something a bit more than that,'' he commented. ''Your mom wanted to know if she should get one room or two ready? Right? A sort of polite way to ask if we were sleeping together?''

''Do you think I'm being foolish?''

Drew smiled. ''I think you're being yourself, sweetheart.''

''It's not as if I make a habit...''

''Darlin','' he assured her, ''you don't owe me any explanations. Now, don't you think it's time you opened your gifts?''

Relieved, Kate leapt up and went to get them, returning a moment later. Maverick and Iceman at her heels, she sat back down. The dogs did likewise, one at her feet, the other at Drew's. Slowly, taking her time, she pulled the dark green velvet ribbon from the one package, carefully opening the matching paper. A long wooden box, with the initials KR swirled into the top, was revealed. Opening the lid, Kate gasped. A set of expensive pens, one fountain, the other ballpoint, were nestled inside the velvet-lined box. They were the color of green marble, and Kate recognized the prestigious maker instantly.

"My God, Drew," she gushed, "they're exquisite."

"When I saw them, I thought of you. The color reminded me of Ireland, and since I know you have a fondness for the country, I couldn't resist."

Kate picked up the fountain pen, examining the engraving on the gold clip. Her name and the date. It was the same on the matching ballpoint.

"What can I say?"

"'Thanks' will suffice," Drew stated more casually than he felt. He was inordinately pleased that this gift had touched her. There was no denying the genuine joy on Kate's face. "Don't forget there's another."

This time Kate was more anxious, ripping the paper with suddenly clumsy fingers. Inside the white box, the name of a famous auction house with branches in several major worldwide cities stamped on the lid, was an antique Victorian cut-glass inkwell with a sterling silver lid, embossed with a cherub's head.

"For your collection."

Kate hefted the weight of it in her palm, marveling at the detail of the craftsmanship. "It's beautiful."

"I'm glad that you like it."

"*Like?*" she asked incredulously. She ran her finger over the raised silver design, tracing the cherub's full face, the curly hair. "I never expected anything like this. *These,*" she corrected herself quickly.

"Which makes it all the more fun, sweetheart. Yes, fun," he responded. "Shopping's not high on my list of things to do in my spare time. However, this was exciting. Like a puzzle, finding something that matched you, that I thought you'd like. That was the incentive for me."

"Well, you've succeeded big-time, I can assure you," Kate stated. She was thrilled. He'd taken the time to select things that would have meaning for her. A man in his position could have picked any impersonal item or hired someone to select a generic gift. That Drew would make an effort on her behalf pleased her more than she cared to admit.

Kate rose from her chair, taking the few short steps that brought her to Drew. Leaning down, she placed a tender kiss on his wide mouth. Before he could react, Kate stepped back, eyes glistening with traces of moisture. "Just let me put these upstairs, then we can go."

His lips curved into a healthy smile as he leaned over to pet Maverick's head as Kate dashed off. "What can I say?" he said to the dog, "I love her." The animal barked, joined by Iceman.

Kate gently laid the items on her desk, handling each one again, her fingers lightly skimming over the pens, the inkwell. She hugged herself, a secret smile kicking up the corners of her lips.

Drew Buchanan was a very special person, indeed.

Their day had been filled with fun. Instead of using Drew's rental car, Kate had driven him around in her comfortable sedan, the reason being she was taking the collies with them. Her "boys" would enjoy the change of scenery as well as they would, she stated.

A good time was had by all, as Kate, camera in hand, stopped occasionally so that the dogs could run and so that she could capture the day on film. Moments that she could take out and relive whenever she wanted.

As she soaked in a hot tub later that afternoon, big enough for two to bathe comfortably, Kate mused on the evening Drew had planned. She still had no idea where he was taking her for dinner. He was being remarkably closemouthed.

She wiggled her toes in the foamy bath water, recalling the photo she'd taken of Drew and her dogs along the Brandywine River. He looked so at home in the shot. As if he belonged here, belonged with her.

Yet, Kate wondered, was that what she *wanted* to see? Did it really exist—or was it only in her fertile imagination?

Every minute, every hour that passed, made her want him more. Every second not spent with him while he was here was wasted; time she couldn't recover.

Why, she asked herself, hadn't she simply invited him to spend the time with her here, in her house? She had two spare bedrooms.

She'd bring it up over dinner tonight. Suggest that he should stop wasting his money and move in with her for the duration of his stay.

Kate laughed out loud at the notion of saving his money. Perhaps that wasn't quite the right approach to take, considering that if he wanted to, Drew could probably buy the inn he was staying at with nary a blink of an eye, or a dent in his trust fund. All the extra zeros on her advance checks probably wouldn't even faze this Texas billionaire.

That thought made Kate smile. At least she was certain he wasn't after her for her *fortune*.

She closed her eyes, daydreams taking over as she relaxed in the still, warm water, fantasizing.

The hands that slid over her skin were strong and sure. She could feel them lifting her, bringing her closer to the male body that shared the space of the tiled whirlpool. Jets of water sluiced under and around her, until she floated on a sea of pure sensation. Her bare limbs tangled with his; her nipples scraped against the crisp dark hair on his wide chest; her arms wound around his neck as their lips met, the kiss deep and satisfying.

He shifted, easing her up and over him until their bodies blended as one. Her short nails dug into his broad shoulders, anchoring her as she rode the crest of their mutual desire, spinning out of control.

Kate's eyes snapped open; her hands eased the grip she had on the wide, flat tiled rim. Her heart pounded.

Expelling a deep, ragged sigh, she rose from the cooling water, stepping up and out of the tub, wiping away the last traces of the bubbles with a brisk rub from the fluffy white towel. She gave a lingering glance at the water, watching as it drained away. Her daydream had seemed so real.

And it could be. All she had to do was act on her fantasy. Let him know she wanted to be with him, in every way.

But something still held her back. Doubts that chained her to the wall of uncertainty. Only she could free herself. Only she could dispel the vestiges of the past.

To do that, she had to be sure of her heart. Very sure.

Maverick and Iceman were barking up a storm.

"What's the problem?" Kate demanded of her pets

as she made her way down the stairs on her high heels. "Hush. It's only Drew."

Only Drew.

She checked herself again in the hall mirror, satisfied with her appearance.

Only Drew. That thought brought a smile to her face. He was more than a mere "only." Drew Buchanan was one of a kind—the man who made her see options. Who brought dreams back into her life.

Kate had selected a dress to match her mood. This birthday, she felt, marked a turning point. It was the first one in three years that she actually looked forward to. It wasn't, as previously, a way to mark time since Jack's death.

Framed family pictures hung on the wall. Kate glanced up, spotting one of her favorites—she and Jack on their honeymoon. *I think you'd like him,* she mentally addressed the photo. *He's a lot like you in some ways.*

A momentary wave of sadness touched her. *If only I could be sure he wouldn't leave me like you did. What do you think, Jack? Can I trust him? I once trusted you with my life—and more important, with your own.*

Kate stared at the gay faces, frozen in time. Happiness could be so ephemeral. *I'm afraid, Jack. So very afraid. What do I do?*

Answer the doorbell, a voice inside her head mocked.

Kate opened the door, surprise widening her blue eyes as she took in the handsome man before her. Drew stood there, formally dressed in a black dinner jacket and trousers, red handkerchief in his breast pocket, pleated white shirt and a thousand-watt smile on his lips. In his large hand he held a long, slim box, which he handed to her. He leaned over and placed a tender salute upon her mouth. "For you," he stated. "Happy birthday, again, sweetheart."

"Come in," she said, lifting the lid on the white floral box. Inside the carefully wrapped green paper, there were a dozen yellow roses. A rich, golden shade as bright as the Texas sun.

Kate bent her head and inhaled the fragrance while Drew hunkered down and greeted the dogs affectionately. "They're beautiful," she murmured.

"Like you," he answered, rising, his gaze taking in every inch of the woman in front of him. God, but she was stunning. A dress of deepest ruby red velvet hugged her body to perfection. Her soft creamy white skin rose temptingly from the off-the-shoulder neckline. Her burnished blond hair was held back by two glittering rhinestone combs, allowing him to feast on the elegant structure of her jawline, the length of her neck. A simple strip of velvet, in the same shade as her dress, adorned with a cameo, was tied around her neck. Small ruby studs decked her ears.

He marked the color in his memory—it suited her.

Cradling the box to her bosom, Kate said, "Let me get a vase and put these in water before we go."

Drew watched as she hurried off to the kitchen, briefly checking the time on his watch. Tonight was a night for wooing, for showing her the best of times; for surprises big and small.

Kate returned, carrying a tall cut-glass vase, the roses resting inside. She placed them on the hall table, once again inhaling the scent.

Her coat was draped over the newel post.

Drew picked it up and helped Kate into it, enfolding her in his arms, his teeth nibbling briefly on her earlobe

"Ready?" he asked, his voice husky and dark, as inviting and alluring as the promise of true love.

"Yes," she whispered in response, letting him lead her outside. It was then that she realized he hadn't driven in his rental car. A long black limousine was parked in her driveway, a uniformed chauffeur waiting by the door, a smile on his face.

"Good evening, ma'am," he said, tipping his hat as he opened the door to the back seat.

"Good evening," Kate automatically replied, sliding into the luxurious interior. A bottle of chilled champagne and two fluted crystal glasses waited, along with every comfort one could want or imagine. She sank into the seat, leather cushioning her body like a glove.

Drew followed her in, shutting the door with a click, sealing them in a world of their own; a darkened glass panel separated them from the driver. He reached over and set about opening the champagne, pouring them each a glass. A muted light bathed them in a warm glow. A button was flipped and vintage rock 'n' roll ballads filled the car.

"I'm impressed," Kate declared honestly, clinking her glass to his in a salute. She'd ridden in a limo before, but this one was in a different class altogether. "You're good for one helluva surprise, Mr. Buchanan."

"To happy birthdays and new beginnings," he proposed, moving closer to her.

Kate smiled and nodded her head, sipping the champagne slowly, her eyes fixed on his. "How about to surprises—of all kinds?"

The bell-like sound of fine crystal pealing against another piece echoed in the air. "To making dreams come true."

"To you and me," she added softly.

With that toast, Drew drained his glass.

"So—" she held out her glass for a refill "—where are you taking me?"

Drew wanted to answer, *directly to bed.* "New York."

Kate almost choked on the champagne she was drinking.

"There's a steakhouse I know of that makes a mean grilled porterhouse, smothered in onions."

Kate slanted him a sly look. "Shall I make an educated guess that it's Texas beef?"

"Only the best, darlin', *Buchanan* beef."

"Chauvinist," she teased.

Drew's grin was infectious. "Guess I'll have to plead guilty, sweetheart." He topped off their glasses. "But I do have to admit that my younger brother Burke raises the best beef in the country, real prime."

"Emma loves the ranch."

"I think you would, too," Drew said, pride heavy in his voice.

Kate realized that she very much wanted to see the place that had spawned the man sitting beside her.

Softly, he whispered in her ear, "Would you come if I asked you?"

She didn't hesitate. "Yes. I'd like to meet the rest of your family."

"It's a big one."

"All the better."

"You might not think that once you've seen the Buchanan clan all together. We can take some getting used to."

"Don't bet on it," she answered. "I told you, I've got relatives galore, too."

Drew risked delving into personal territory. "What about kids?"

Kate licked her lips, taking refuge in a sip of the champagne. "What about them?"

"Do you like them?" He tilted her chin up and around so that she faced him. "Do you regret not having any?"

"Yes to both questions."

He saw the bittersweet sadness that momentarily clouded her eyes. Responding to instinct, Drew put his glass down, took hers and dispatched it also, gathering her into his arms, snuggling her close. Kate's head rested on his chest and her arms slipped about him. "I'm sorry if I brought up painful things."

"It's not like I haven't given the matter some thought before," she admitted. "But then I realized that neither my husband nor myself was ready to handle that responsibility at that time." She turned the question back at him. "What about you?"

"Truthfully, I never gave it much thought before." And he hadn't—a family of his own had meant ties; it meant claims on his life, his time. A loss of personal autonomy. Love, however, had changed that perception. Through his younger brother's eyes, Drew had seen it as an extension of self, of the love that Burke shared with Emma. An addition rather than a subtraction. Holding that wonderful new life in his hands, Drew realized that parenthood wasn't a burden; it was, or could be, a blessing, a confirmation of life and renewal.

Before what? she'd wanted to ask.

"Though I've gotta admit to feeling mighty happy around my niece and nephew," he added. "They can make a man reconsider the notion of having a family of his own quicker than a rattlesnake can strike."

Family. The word buzzed in her head even as she

laughed at his words. "That's a wild analogy there, pardner."

"Stick with me, sweetheart, I've got more where that came from."

It was a magical night, complete with special delights and even more surprises.

The restaurant he'd picked was charming; expecting one thing, Kate found another. Small rather than huge and boisterous; the antithesis of wild and woolly.

Drew arranged everything, from their food and wine, to the dessert, a luscious birthday cake, made and decorated especially for her, the rest of which was now reposing in her kitchen under a glass cake dome.

She lifted the lid, smiling at the white chocolate frosting covered with a border of yellow roses.

In less than eight hours she'd see him again.

Kate thought back to their good-night kiss. It was filled with promise, ripe with the prospects of fulfillment. Veering past tender, it went all the way to hot and hungry, arousing each of them to take it further.

When Drew stepped back, he was breathing heavily. "Damn, but I do like kissing you, sweetheart. So much so that it pains me to have to quit." He ran one finger down her flushed cheek. "But if I don't stop now, then I won't be able to, and you're not ready yet tonight to take it any further, are you?"

She wanted to beg him to stay. To tell him to send the driver on his way and come inside with her, carry her up those stairs. Share her bed tonight and all the nights that followed.

"I wish..."

"Hush," he whispered, his voice low and raw with desire. "I can wait."

"Are you sure?"

"If I wasn't, then I wouldn't be here. I told you, dar-lin', I'm not going anywhere just yet. You're worth the wait."

Worth the wait.

Kate hoped so. It wasn't fair to keep him hanging while she worked through her uncertainty. Soon, she'd have to make up her mind and give him an answer, one way or the other.

With a flick of her index finger, Kate scooped up a confectionery rose, popped it into her mouth, sucking off all traces of the frosting.

Kate licked her lips, savoring the taste. *Sweet.*

The way love had once been for her.

The way, if she wanted, it could be again.

All she had to do was take the chance.

Chapter Twelve

Iceman and Maverick raced along the beach, chasing sea gulls, while Kate strolled at a more sedate pace with Drew. Arms around each other, they walked in silence across the long stretch of sand.

Inhaling the sharp tang of the ocean, Kate paused, turning to look out over the waves as they tumbled toward them, breaking down, dissolving upon contact with the shore. Drew slid his arms around her waist, molding his bigger body to hers. Kate leaned back, her head resting casually on his chest. She felt relaxed, comfortable and strangely at peace. As if she'd finally found a sweet, safe place, balanced between the past and the future.

It was late afternoon, the sun hanging low in the sky, providing a surprising amount of warmth on this autumn day. There was a gentle breeze blowing in from the water. Dunes dotted the landscape, tufts of wild grass sticking up like spikes. Gulls called to one another overhead, flying nearby in their eternal search for food.

Drew was content to simply hold Kate. Her body felt right in his arms; the same way her presence felt right in his life. Last night had been wonderful. The trip to New York had been a huge success. The hardest part had been leaving her alone at her house and returning back to his solitary room at the inn. Slipping below the sheet and comforter there, he'd longed to feel the touch of her skin close to his. Wished for the smell of her perfume to waft through his nostrils. Wanted to experience once more the pure, unabashed way she made love—giving herself over to the act with unbridled abandon, changing his expectations, giving him a new and different way to dream.

"I'm glad that you brought me here," he murmured, his voice a soft caress to her ears.

She could willingly listen to that dulcet voice for the next fifty years, never getting bored. "So am I," she answered, her hands crossed over his. Snuggled so close to him, contentment filled Kate, along with the realization that she longed to be there, in his embrace. Her brain and body tingled anew with the sensation of coming back to life. As if somehow she'd been partially frozen in her widowhood, buried under layers of frost to protect her heart from further violation. She couldn't ignore the heat he possessed, from his smoldering glance to his fiery kisses; from the fervid, totally impassioned way he made love—as if they were the only male and female that existed; as if every moment were doubly precious because he was sharing it with her.

Drew had given her something she hadn't been aware of lacking—hope. Faith in the future, coupled with the knowledge that she could once again come alive in a man's arms.

"I like it here."

Kate angled her head, looking backward. "Do you?" A wavy, wayward lock of hair had fallen onto his wide forehead, curling temptingly.

"Yeah. It's kinda different being in a place like this when the weather's cool. Beaches, at least for me, are destinations to escape to when the weather turns foul. Have you ever been to the Caribbean, or Hawaii, when winter's got its tenacious grip on the temperature?"

"No," she answered. Such a mention conjured up pictures of Drew on the sandy beaches of some exotic address. Sunlight strong and hot, beating down on him, turning his skin a warm shade of dark gold. Stripped down, a mere scrap of clothing preserving his modesty; or perhaps a more casual approach, loose boxer-type shorts. Still, Kate imagined the feel of his chest under her fingertips, hair-roughened flesh warmed by the sun. Or the scent of his skin, saltier than normal to the taste. Or maybe they would swim in the moonlight, the sea an inviting touch to their bare bodies.

He wondered what she was thinking. One minute she was there with him, the next there was a faraway look in her eyes as she turned her head and once again gazed out into the ocean.

Drew kissed the top of Kate's head, her hair responding to the change in the temperature and excessive moisture—it curled even more. "That's when I enjoy it the most," he said, getting back to the subject. "But there's something to be said for your take on it. That gray-green shade of the Atlantic. Salt air mixed with a dash of chilliness. The beach all to ourselves. The perfect spot for making a picnic."

"Picnic? At this time of year?"

"Where's your spirit of adventure, darlin'?" he teased. "A blanket, something warm to drink, something hot to eat and a fire." He brushed aside a wave of her hair and kissed her neck. "Could prove interesting."

With him, it would be heaven, Kate decided. Drew was the kind of man willing to try new things, garner new experiences. His mind, as well as his body, enthralled her. Life with him would never be dull or commonplace. He had a special way of making her breathe deeper, see clearer, feel stronger.

"I might be persuaded to give it a try sometime," she said provocatively, "if I had the right incentive."

"Such as?"

Kate turned her head and let the corners of her mouth gently kick up. "I'll let you figure that out for yourself."

Drew's reply was a hearty laugh. Damn if she didn't throw more curves than a Texas all-star pitcher. Calm and cool one minute, hot and steamy another. A living paradox who captivated him as no one woman ever had; or, he was confident, ever would again. He supposed family legend was true—Buchanan males in love *were* one-woman men. He'd sure enough found his.

"I guess we should be heading back." Kate slipped around so that she was facing Drew. She reached up and framed the lower part of his face with her hands. Standing on tiptoe, she positioned a soft, fleeting kiss on his mouth. "Thank you," she murmured, blue eyes staring longingly into brown.

"For what?"

"For just being who you are."

A big, Texas-size grin, deepening the grooves on either side of his mouth, appeared on Drew's face. "Happy to oblige, ma'am," he drawled.

"Okay, pardner," she said, playing along with his down-home persona, "let's round up them doggies and head on back to the homestead." Kate gave a loud whistle that got the collies' attention. They came bounding back across the expanse of sand to where the couple stood. "I think 'cookie' will have supper ready by now."

"Yes, ma'am. We'd better be makin' tracks so's not to get her riled up. Nothing's more upsettin' than a good cook on a rip-roarin' tear. Why, folks been known to gather their saddlebags and vamoose for less."

Kate laughed along with him, adding, "Don't give up your day job, pardner."

Drew smiled, the dogs walking beside them, fresh from their romp. He supposed that the time would soon come when he should tell Kate that that's just what he'd done. Given up the roaming, often frenzied life of a journalist for a chance to linger, to put down roots. It might make a difference in their courtship. Or, then again, it might not. What he really wanted to know was that she'd made a choice for him, not for what might happen. Accepted who and what he was, job and all, as he accepted everything she was.

But first he had to get past the few remaining walls that separated them. Something else had to be resolved—he just wished that he knew what it was. Something that lingered in Kate's eyes, in her voice, in her manner; it lingered beneath the surface. What was it? He thought that he'd managed to rebuild the feelings that they'd shared in San Antonio. The chemistry between them was still there, better than before. He woke up thinking about her; he went to sleep with her face the last thing on his mind.

Perhaps it was time to push the envelope a bit further?

Stir up the elements and hope that he wasn't spitting in the wind.

"You really do like that young man, don't you," Kate's mother asked as she placed another freshly washed stainless steel pot into the dish drainer.

Kate dried the last piece of her mother's good china. Her "special occasion pieces" Janet Reeves called them. A smile curved Kate's mouth before she answered. "Yes."

Janet Reeves nodded knowingly. "I could tell. It's in the way you look at him."

"Is it that obvious, eh?"

Wiping her wet hands on a nearby floral towel, Janet hugged her daughter. "To me, it is," she confided. "Don't forget, I know you, darling. All too well. And," she added, setting the kettle on for a pot of tea, "I can still remember how it was between you and Jack."

"So can I."

Her mother recognized the almost agonized look that passed over her daughter's face. "What's the matter?"

Kate decided to confide in her mother, explaining the situation to her, all of it. How and where she and Drew had met, what happened between them. She was remarkably frank, wanting to hear her mother's take on the subject.

Janet Reeves listened quietly while her daughter spoke, fixing the large pot of tea as Kate poured out the complete story of her short-lived affair with Drew Buchanan.

Kate sighed. "I just don't know if I can go through that again."

"Go through what?"

"Worrying. Waiting for it to happen again."

"*It?*" Janet asked.

"You know, Mom, the *call.* Drew's a journalist. A damned good one, believe me. Some of the stories he covers are hot. *Too* hot. Dangerous."

Janet realized the problem her daughter faced. "You're afraid that one day he won't come back. Like Jack, right?"

"Yes," Kate responded, bunching the wet dish towel in her hands. "Like Jack."

"You married Jack knowing he was a cop."

"Yes, I did," Kate readily admitted. "I gambled that when he went through the door in the morning that he would be coming back through it the same night." She hung the dish towel over the wooden rack to dry. "Being a good cop was all that Jack ever wanted. It's what his father and uncle were, as well as one of his brothers. A cop was who he was."

"You accepted that."

"I did," Kate agreed.

"Honey, I think I can safely say that they're two different men."

"Only in some ways, Mom," Kate argued. "In others, they're like brothers under the skin. That's what frightens me. I love that man sitting in the den with Daddy. And that's something I wouldn't have believed possible less than a year ago. I thought that when Jack died, the part of me that loved in that way shut down, that it wouldn't be resurrected again. All I wanted from Drew Buchanan in San Antonio was sex," she said bluntly. "I got that."

"And something else. Something you hadn't counted on, right?" Janet's gray-blue eyes homed in on her daughter's blue orbs.

A small, ironic smile kicked up the corners of Kate's

mouth. "Don't they say that fools rush in? Yeah," she said. "I found love again."

"A lot of people don't get a second chance, honey."

"I know that."

"Are you willing to toss that aside?" Janet came closer. "What is it you want?"

"Security. Guarantees. No repeats of the past. Is that too much to ask?"

"Of course not," her mother assured her. "We'd all like that. It's human nature." Mother and daughter exchanged hugs. "I can't tell you how to live your life. Besides, I think you're doing well enough on your own."

"But?"

"I'm proud of you, Kate. You've made your personal dream come true—you're a success in your chosen endeavor. You've had a deep and wonderful love. Unfortunately, it didn't last as long as you'd—we'd all— hoped. Jack was a good man. I can't begin to understand why he was taken from you so soon. I probably never will. But he was. It wasn't fair. You two had your whole lives together."

Bitterly, Kate said, "Until an abusive man high on crack changed the plans."

"You're young. Life has given you another opportunity for happiness, if you truly want it." Janet poured the steeping hot tea into elegant china cups, which she placed on a simple pine tray. She added a plateful of her homemade shortbread. "I wouldn't," she cautioned her child, "spit in the face of fortune."

"Meaning, you think that I should go with the flow?"

Janet chuckled at her child's words, breaking the tension. "I think you should go with your heart. At best, it's the only thing you can trust. If you don't, you may regret it. Talk to him. Explain your fears.'' She added a stack of decorated paper napkins, which matched the autumn-theme-designed paper plates. ''You never said, is he comfortable with you earning so much money? I mean, some men would be apt to be intimidated by your income.''

It was Kate's turn to chuckle. ''Drew isn't bothered by my making money, Mom. Trust me. It's not a factor.''

''That's good.'' Janet Reeves sliced a lemon into wedges. ''Even though he's rich, it's still nice to have money of one's own.''

''Drew's even read my books,'' Kate stated. ''Can you believe it? He likes them. In fact, I'd go so far as to say that he's proud of me.''

Her mother gave Kate a hug. ''What's not to be proud of? You're a terrific writer.''

''There speaks the unbiased mother.''

''Unbiased, hell,'' she declared. ''I'm thrilled with your success, just as proud as I am of my other children and the choices they've made.''

''Thanks, Mom.''

''None needed, honey. It's the truth.'' Janet gave her tray a last glance. ''Is he okay with paper, or should I stick with cotton napkins?''

Kate reassured her mom. ''Drew's no snob. From what Emma's told me, the whole family is sort of on the relaxed side. You know, comfortable with the wealth. The one who's the most formal would probably be, from what Emma's indicated, the eldest Buchanan brother, Clay.''

''He's the one that wanted to marry Emma first, right?''

Kate nodded her head.

"Does he look like Drew?"

"I don't think so. I haven't met him. Burke and Drew are a lot alike, however. Both tall and dark, though Drew's got about three inches or so on his brother. Slightly bigger body frame, too. Burke appears to be the strong, silent type. Drew's more loquacious, more comfortable in social situations."

"I must admit that your fellow's quite nice-looking."

Kate smiled. "He is, isn't he? That's the first thing about him that caught my eye. He strode through that crowd on the River Walk, secure and confident, looking like he belonged on the cover of a men's fashion magazine, or better yet," she added dreamily, resting her elbows on the butcher-block island table, "one of my books.

"He'd be an improvement over some that I could name," Kate added. "With that twinkle in his beautiful brown eyes, and that wicked grin, he could be anything from a buccaneer to a cowboy, an aristocrat to a scoundrel."

Janet patted one of Kate's hands. "You do have it bad, my dear."

Kate shrugged. "Guess you're right, Mom."

"I played some ball in high school and college," Drew said in response to the question asked by Kate's father. They were sitting in the large family room of the seashore house, watching a college football game on the wide-screen TV. "What about you?"

"Much the same," the older man stated. "Broke my shoulder in senior year of college, so I didn't finish the year. Stood me in good stead, though, as I got to spend more time with a certain sophomore student."

"Kate's mother?"

Adam Reeves answered with a slightly smug smile.

"I take it that you've been together ever since, then?"

"Except for a stint for Uncle Sam in the army, yes."

"My parents are the same," Drew informed him. "Known each other all their lives. Not surprising, since they're distant cousins."

Adam lowered the sound on the remote. "Do you mind my asking where you're from? Your accent's faint, but it definitely isn't East Coast." He stroked his chin. "I'd hazard a guess at somewhere in the West."

"Texas."

Adam nodded his head. "Always wanted to see that place. I roomed one year at college with a guy from Lufkin."

"Nice town," Drew commented. "I've been there before, when I was a boy to visit a relative. Second or third cousin, I think, on my mother's side."

"Come from a big family, do you, son?"

Drew grinned. He could well imagine that the Buchanan family tree, with all its multifarious branches, would be mind-blowing for Kate's dad. It was, at times, boggling to those already in the family. "Big enough."

Adam nodded. "Family's a good thing to have. Helps you get through the rough times."

"Kate told me that it was a help to her when her first husband died."

Adam Reeves wondered if the man had made a slip with the word *first*. Far as he knew, Jack was his daughter's *only* husband, unless this man was looking to become number two.

"Yeah, that was rough for my girl," her father stated. "The Terrellis were a big part of helping her cope, too. They're good people." Adam picked up the remote and flicked the channel to another all-sports cable network while halftime of the game commenced. "So, you're a journalist, I understand. Write for a newspaper?"

"No, a magazine." Drew named the Texas monthly that he'd worked for for the past eight years, giving Kate's father some background to the kinds of stories he'd done.

"That how you met Katie?"

"She's a good friend of my sister-in-law's. Emma introduced us while Kate was visiting my brother and his wife in San Antonio in June."

"She married a rancher, if I recall correctly. Katie told her mom and me about it early this year."

"That she did. My younger brother, Burke."

"You live on the ranch?"

Drew shook his head. "San Antonio's home for me, when I'm there, that is."

"So, then, you're just visiting up here?"

Drew recognized the concern in the older man's voice. "Sort of." At that moment, he decided to confide in her dad about his plans. "I'm hoping to persuade your daughter to marry me."

Beneath his bushy salt-and-pepper brows, Adam's blue eyes were sharp. "You are?"

"If she'll have me, then yes, I most certainly am."

Adam leaned back in his comfortable, overstuffed chair. "You're in love with my Katie?"

Drew looked the other man square in the eye. "If you'll pardon me for saying it this way, damn straight I am."

Adam searched the younger man's face, attempting to read it. Drew appeared sincere, but Adam had to be sure, even if he risked alienating the Texan. Pointedly, Adam asked, "My girl's quite successful in her profession, but then again, I suppose that you're already aware of that fact?"

"Well aware, sir." Drew smiled, recognizing the implicit question behind the words. "You want to know if her money makes Kate easier to love? Trust me," he stated, "I couldn't care less about it."

"That's easy to say now," Adam Reeves proposed. "Another matter once the wedding ring is on her finger."

Drew wasn't used to his integrity being questioned. Ordinarily, he would have bristled at the suggestion that he would go after a woman for her money. However, he could well understand Kate's father's concerns. This man didn't know who he was. Whether or not he was spinning a web of lies to trap a vulnerable young woman.

"Sir," Drew began, "let me tell you a bit about my family and my ability to take care of your daughter financially, should she want that." Drew calmly and succinctly filled the older man in on his finances. "That should alleviate any worries you might have about money. Ask Kate. She knows."

Adam's face reddened in embarrassment. "*Those* Buchanans." He had vaguely heard of the family. A moment later he broke into a deep smile. "Well, I wish you luck, then. Katie knows her own mind. Always has." Adam offered his hand to the younger man, confiding, "I'm glad to see my girl's face filled with happiness once again. It's been far too long. I'd hazard a guess that you're responsible for that."

"I hope I am," Drew responded. "So, I've got your blessing, then?"

Adam Reeves was touched by the old-fashioned gesture. "Long as you make her happy, son, you'll always have my blessing."

"It won't be for lack of trying, sir."

"What won't be for lack of trying?" Kate asked as she entered the room with her mother, setting the tea tray down on the square wooden coffee table. She took a seat next to Drew on the couch, and his arm slid around her shoulders, pulling her close to his body. Drew didn't hesitate to give her a quick kiss.

Behind them, Kate's parents shared a knowing glance, both beaming at the couple.

"You're going to ignore my question, aren't you?" Kate asked softly.

Drew leaned over and picked up a cup of hot tea, squeezing a wedge of chilled lemon into it and added a heaping teaspoon of sugar. "You know me so well."

"Do I?" she shot back, then picked up one of the shortbread fingers, snapped it in two and popped the smallest piece into her mouth.

"None better, sweetheart."

"Hmm" was her muffled reply.

"It looked as though you and my dad were getting along quite well," Kate said as she reentered the room. Her parents had gone to bed about a half hour before, and Kate had taken the remains of their tea to the kitchen and cleaned up.

"We were. He loves you very much." Drew watched her walk around the room, her movements smooth and fluid and, to him, so sexy that he thought he would explode from wanting her. It was all he could do to sit here.

"The feeling's mutual." She stopped in front of the stereo, bending down to open the cabinets and sort through the contents. Holding a 45-rpm record in her hand, she turned slightly and held it up. "Recognize this?"

"I should. We've got plenty at our house and at the ranch. My parents won't throw them away."

"Neither will mine. I used to love to go through their collection and listen to the oldies, especially Motown." Kate flipped through the stack. "'My Guy.' I loved that song."

Kate laughed. "I thought it was a hoot when they used it in the movie *Sister Act.* So clever." She replaced the record, realizing that now she found a deeper, more poignant message in the lyrics.

Kate turned her head, her glance a silent invitation to Drew.

He rose fluidly from the couch, joining her. Having removed his shoes, he walked soundlessly over the bare expanse of hardwood floor.

"I used to like to riffle through the British invasion stuff. You know, the Beatles and the Stones. Do you see 'Satisfaction' in there?"

Kate shot him a quick look, trying to gauge his mood. "'Fraid not."

"Pity."

She wet her lips. "But I've got a few things here that are danceable."

"Put them on," he instructed softly.

Kate did and held out her arms to him, pushing out of her sneakers so that she, too, was in her socks.

Drew didn't hesitate to take her up on the invitation. "You sure this isn't going to have your parents coming down to check?" The incongruity of the situation almost made him laugh out loud, as if they were teenagers instead of the adults that they really were.

"I'll keep it low."

They melted into each other, their bodies blending and shifting with the rhythm of the music. Slowly, they glided around the floor, content to sway back and forth.

Drew picked a safe topic, trying to keep his mind off the fact that the woman he loved was in his arms and he wanted her, desperately. "What did your folks do?"

Kate, her head comfortably resting on Drew's chest, answered, "They were teachers. Mom still is, though part-time now at a local adult education center as a volunteer. Dad retired, and he gardens now. That's his passion. He helped Jack and me plan the gardens for my house."

"What did they teach?"

"Mom taught American history at Crestview Academy for Girls, not far from where I live now. Dad taught English literature at the local public high school."

"So, you come by your passion for writing naturally," he suggested. "A combination of both your parents' subjects."

"I suppose so," Kate agreed.

"Language skills and a historian's eye." Drew came to a stop, looking down at her suddenly upturned face. God help him, he couldn't resist or ignore his feelings any longer. Bending, he scooped her up and brought her to the couch.

Drew wrapped his arms about Kate as she snuggled closer to his big, warm body.

Neither one could resist the kiss that was inevitable. They were drawn together, unable to break the link that had only grown stronger. Temporarily surrendering to the moment, they made the most of it, seeking the satisfaction of lips taking lips.

Raw passion, simmering beneath the surface, broke through and rose to the top.

"Help me get this off," Kate whispered brokenly, indicating her pullover navy sweater.

Drew obliged, sending the garment to the floor. He unbuttoned the top four buttons of her blue oxford shirt, exposing the creamy skin underneath. Sensing her compliance, he loosened several more, until they were all undone.

He raised his head, then dipped it. His mouth covered one cotton-clad nipple, tongue-laving it to a stiff peak.

Kate's moans were low, coming from deep in her throat.

Drew transferred his attention to her other breast, giving it the same consideration.

Her hands had a will of their own, rising and pulling his head toward her eager mouth. His hair was like raw silk. His dark eyes were intense. "Kiss me," she demanded.

It was hot and devouring, direct and wet, taking them rapidly out of control.

It took all of Drew's iron self-will to pull back. He gasped air into his lungs, watching as Kate did the same. A moment passed before he could speak, and when he did, his voice was a raspy growl. "Kate, I want you. That should be obvious."

"It is—and I want *you*." She turned her head, glancing around the room. "You don't have to continue. I know what you're going to say. I agree."

He kissed her tenderly. "I wish..."

"So do I."

"We've got things to resolve."

"Uh-huh."

"And I don't feel all that comfortable doing it here when there's a chance..."

She let out a giggle, which broke the tension. "Neither do I."

"Then how about we cut this visit short and go back home tomorrow?"

Home. Kate discovered she liked the sound of that word on his lips. She hastily rebuttoned her shirt. "Whatever you say."

Drew grinned as he pushed himself backward so that he was sitting instead of lying on the couch. "I sure as hell know what I'd like to say, darlin'."

As if she'd read his mind, Kate responded, "It goes double for me."

Drew rose. "Excuse me, ma'am, but I think I need to take a shower before I turn in." He slanted a steamy glance in her direction. "A very long, very *cold* shower."

"Sounds like a grand idea. I think I'll do the same."

Chapter Thirteen

Kate sat sipping coffee on the deck of her parents' house, her thoughts lingering on last evening. Drew, her father had informed her, was up early and had taken the dogs for a walk along the beach.

She nibbled on a slice of toast liberally spread with orange marmalade, wishing that she'd awakened in his arms instead of by herself. It was all she could do to stop from pulling him into a broom closet and having her wicked way with him, such was the power of the fierce attraction between them.

There could be no doubts about that in her mind. Drew wanted her as much as she wanted him. Hadn't he said that he was anxious to explore their relationship? So far, they'd kept a pretty tight rein on their passion, allowing nothing to get out of hand. The time they'd spent together had been congenial and cautious, neither of them breaking the barrier to full intimacy.

She loved him.

But what about Drew? Did he feel as deeply? No words of love had so far passed his lips. That he desired her, Kate was certain. He yearned for what they'd shared in San Antonio as much as she. Last night, had they been at her house, they would have made love.

Parting from him after that episode had been almost unbearable, especially knowing he slept just across the hall from her room. She'd lain awake, missing him, forcing herself to remain in her bed, when all she wanted was within reach.

When she finally fell asleep, Kate was plagued by dreams, each one more erotic than the previous.

One she remembered vividly this morning had been especially sexy.

She'd been standing in the den, sifting through the assorted stack of 45s in a long, flowing nightgown of heavy satin in a copper brown shade. It hugged her bare body like a slip, slit up one side to her upper thigh. She was waiting. Watching. But for what? Or whom? She really wasn't sure.

It was dark. The only illumination was from one small lamp in the room and the soft glow of the moon, which bathed the redwood deck in a silvery light.

From out of the shadows came a man. Tall. Dark. Dressed in a black T-shirt and tight black jeans, wearing a smile as wide as the diameter of Texas.

He beckoned for her to come to him.

She took a halting step, then another. She got close to the French doors, pausing within a foot away. He was tempting her—calling to her. Even though she was inside and he outside, the doors locked between them, she could hear the husky way he spoke her name.

His words echoed inside her head. ''You know you

want to join me. Why are you hesitating?'' It was a deeply sexy voice, the kind that could make butter melt. ''Take that final step. Cross the gateway, enter into my world. The world you *want*.''

Her footsteps faltered. She froze, unable to take another step.

''What are you waiting for?'' he demanded, palm out, gesturing for her to meet him. ''You want me. You want this. Admit it.''

''Yes.''

''Then come.''

''I can't.''

''Won't,'' he mocked.

''No!'' she protested. ''I want to. Really.''

''Then what's stopping you?''

''You are.''

He uttered a dark expression of disbelief. ''You summoned me. It was by your will that I came at all.''

She let out a small gasp. ''No.''

''Yes,'' he insisted. ''Do it.'' His voice was seductive. ''Take a few more steps and open the door for me.''

She tried again, managing one more step. Glass and fear separated them.

''Leave me,'' she pleaded. ''I've changed my mind.''

''No, you haven't,'' he persisted.

''Yes, I have.''

''Liar,'' he retorted. ''Tell me you don't want me. Tell me that you aren't as eager for us to be together as I am. Tell me you don't need this as much as I do.'' He paused. ''Can't, can you?'' he taunted. ''I thought not. Let me in.''

She stood immobile.

The next thing she knew the doors were smashed—

broken from the force of his foot kicking them open. Glass shattered; wood splintered.

And then he was there. His greedy mouth on hers, transporting her into a dizzying glimpse of bliss with the power of his deep soul kiss. She surrendered, glorying in the energy she felt rush through her.

"You see, I was right. You do want this and me."

She grabbed his T-shirt, heard it tear as she ripped it. Covering his wide chest with kisses, she fell to her knees.

And then he vanished. Disappeared as if he were merely a figment of the night, leaving her alone and lonely in the moonlight. Hungry. Frustrated.

Emptiness clawed at her insides. Tears fell down her cheeks.

Kate had awoken then, dawn barely breaking in the sky behind the sheer white curtains. The dream had been so real her body still throbbed, bereft of release, for comfort.

Her once-upon-a-time Texas lover had made her ache both in heart and body.

But Drew was right. Here wasn't the place. Last night wasn't the time. Soon, though.

While Kate had questions about their future, she had none about their present. They were leaving this morning, returning to her home to have their long-awaited reckoning. It was useless to postpone the inevitable any longer, not when ardor threatened to erupt whenever they were in the same room.

And it was inevitable. Every kiss, every touch, every glance, brought them closer, stirred memories that had refused to die.

Afterward, they could take time to talk about how far and where this relationship was going.

"Would you care for more coffee?"

Kate turned her head. Her mother was standing in the open French door, a white thermos carafe in her hands.

"Please." Kate held out her cup as her mother closed the door behind her and joined her daughter on the deck.

"You're leaving soon?" Janet asked as she refilled the mug.

"Drew and I have a lot of things to work out, and I thought, why wait?" She shifted in her seat, casting a glance toward the beach. It was colder today. Crisp and clear, like her resolve.

"I think that's a good idea," her mother said. "As much as I love having you, or any of my children, here, and you know that I do, honey, it's important for you to get the situation settled satisfactorily."

"You're right." Kate took another sip of the hot liquid. "I don't need any more time to know that Drew and I get along splendidly. That's a given. What I need to know is if we'll suit together, if there's something we can build on." She edged one jeans-clad leg up, resting her free arm around her knee. "If I can fully accept all the things I cannot change." Kate put down her mug and reached her hand across to her mother's. "And if I can't, what then?"

Drew tossed two pieces of driftwood, watching as the collies chased after them, barking and frolicking. Further along the shore, he saw a couple, arm-in-arm, strolling, stopping every few steps to steal a kiss from each other.

Their actions served to remind him of last night.

It was a good thing that they were going back to Kate's house. Drew doubted that he could keep up this self-imposed ban on lovemaking much longer. Tearing himself away from her last night had been tough. Relinquishing what he wanted most was taking a toll on him. He was through with this on and off, hot and cold, back and forth. Matters had to be faced and dealt with. He couldn't hold back any longer on how he truly felt. He loved Kate. And she had a right to know. Taking the slow and easy path obviously wasn't working as well as he'd planned.

She'd probably be shocked when he told her the truth, considering he'd never made a secret in the past of wanting to remain free and clear of entanglements. All that had changed when he met her. She was the key to the future, unlocking happiness, unlocking the rest of his life.

He felt alive. With Kate he was in love a whole new way. Vibrantly so. Love had lain dormant within him, waiting for the woman who could ignite the passion, tear off the sterile emotional wrappers of his life.

Kate was that woman. The only woman.

Could he convince her of that fact?

He had to.

"How lovely," Kate exclaimed, bending to sniff the floral bouquet that had just arrived from a local shop. The colorful arrangement of flowers was set in a brilliant, golden cut-glass vase, sunlight hitting the edges and sending back sparks of fire. "Who's it from?" she asked.

Janet Reeves opened the card, smiling as she read the message. She handed the note to her daughter. "Guess."

The answer was in the widening of Kate's eyes. "Drew," she murmured. She scanned the card, pleased at his thoughtfulness.

Dear Mrs. Reeves,
A little something to say thank you for your hospitality. Someday I'd like to return the favor.

Drew Buchanan

"How very sweet of him," Janet said appreciatively.

Kate's fingers absently caressed the words on the card. "Yes, wasn't it?"

"I really do like him."

Kate smiled, happy to hear her mother's words. "So do I."

"What's this?" Adam inquired, entering the den and spying the box, which lay on the coffee table along with the crinkly floral paper.

"A gift from Kate's *friend*," his wife answered. "Have a look."

He did, then shot a quick glance at his daughter. *"Interesting,"* he said.

"Daddy—" Kate began.

"He's serious, if you ask me," Adam stated, examining the item closely, pleased with the choice of blooms the arrangement contained, baby's breath and peach-hued Oceania roses.

"I hope so."

"I'm glad to hear you say that," her father responded. "I like him."

"So does Mom."

Adam put one arm around his daughter's shoulders. "Sometimes people get lucky only once in their life and find the one person that makes sense with them." He looked at his wife. "A very few are touched twice. It's up to you, Katie, to decide if you're one of that few."

"I know."

"Personally, I think you may be. But that's only my

opinion, mind you. You'll have to search your heart to find the answer for yourself.''

"I have been.''

"Good. Your mother and I didn't raise any fools.''

"That's for sure,'' Janet stated.

The sound of barking dogs alerted them to the fact that Drew had returned. Kate turned and looked out toward the deck. Suddenly, she felt her heart jump at the sight of Drew hunkered down, wiping off the collies' paws with a towel, so that they wouldn't track sand inside the house. She watched as the dogs licked his face and begged shamelessly to be petted.

Right then and there, Kate knew she couldn't imagine life without him in it.

She slipped away from her folks and joined Drew outside.

"Hi, there.''

His head snapped around and he rose, tossing the towel onto the deck's redwood railing. "Hi, yourself, sweetheart.''

Kate bent down and gave each dog a hug, ruffling fur and whispering a greeting. "I see that you've been a busy guy already. These two will put you through your paces if you're not careful.''

"Nonsense. I think I can handle them.''

"Oh, really?'' she asked, eyebrows raised.

"Sweetheart, they're already eatin' out of my hand.''

"Must be that Texas charm. Or maybe it's a male thing.''

"Could be. I think that animals can generally recognize right away those individuals who they can bond with. It takes people a little longer.''

"People have more things to work through.''

"Excess baggage." His voice was softer. "Sometimes I've found that you have to trust your gut reaction."

"And what if it proves wrong?"

He lifted her chin with two of his fingers. "And what if it doesn't?"

They drove to her house, surprisingly relaxed on the return journey. They'd even stopped to pick up some grocery items at the local supermarket. Drew was content to wait in the car and keep the dogs company while Kate quickly perused the shelves for what she needed.

She found it was fun shopping again for more than one, thinking about what someone else would like to eat. As she wheeled her cart along the aisles, she added things she thought might please Drew.

She'd tempt him with a good dinner, then for dessert...

Her smile was Machiavellian.

A quarter of an hour later, they were pulling up to her drive, Drew jumping out to collect the two days' worth of mail from her box.

When he came back, his arms were loaded with mail, magazines, newspapers and a large, beat-up Jiffy bag. "Looks like it's from your publisher," he said as he read the return address.

"Probably my galley pages for the new book. It never fails. They always come right when I'm almost done with another book." She laughed. "Hopefully, there's also an envelope from my agent. It's royalty time, as well."

"Your check is in the mail," he quipped.

"Ah, yes, the best words in the English language to a writer."

"The best, really?" he queried, slanting her a glance.

"Can you think of any others that mean as much?"

Drew found he could. "What about, *I love you*?"

Kate stopped herself from slamming on her brakes. "Excuse me?" Cautiously, she pulled the sedan into the lane that led to the two-car garage.

"I think you heard me correctly."

"But what did you mean?"

"Exactly what I said. You asked me if there were any other words that could be better than those dealing with money. I gave them to you."

The dogs whined to be let out. Kate hit the button that released the door locks and reached behind her to open the door for the tricolored collie. Drew did the same for the golden dog. They scampered away from the couple, bounding across the lawn.

Of all the places for someone to say I love you, Kate mused.

Well, she guessed it wasn't the first time a man had uttered those words while in a car. Usually though, it was in the back seat and not while having a casual conversation.

"At a loss?" he asked.

"Did you mean it?"

"Sweetheart, I never say things I don't mean. You can take that to the bank, along with your check. Believe it."

Oddly enough, Kate did. He loved her.

"Do you want to sit here or shall we go inside?"

"I think that would be best," she replied, turning off the engine and getting out of the car.

Grocery bags in either arm, she fit her key into the lock of her kitchen door and rushed inside, depositing the paper bags on the table. She was followed into the room by Drew.

He closed the door and turned around. Their eyes met, each unable to sever the connection.

"I want to make love to you," he stated clearly.

"So," she asked, letting everything she'd started to remove from the grocery bags fall back onto the table unheeded, "what are you waiting for?"

It was all the invitation that Drew needed. Uncaring if there was anything breakable in his bags, he let them fall to the floor, the contents spilling out. Things clattered, but neither cared.

They were in each other's arms, lips locked passionately.

"Here?"

"Upstairs," she whispered, "my room."

Drew, his hands at her waist, lifted her. "Hang on, darlin'," he murmured. Kate's legs wrapped around his slim hips as her arms slid around his neck as he made his way to the stairs.

"Where?" he asked, as he reached the second floor.

Kate gave him directions, and seconds later they were in her room and on her bed. Immediately they kissed, touched, straining toward each other.

"Let me take this slow. I've waited so long," he said, his baritone voice sounding even huskier than normal.

"Slow?" Kate remarked in a puzzled tone.

"Yes." Drew kissed her eyelids, her cheeks, the pert tip of her nose, the curve of her cheeks, the sleek line of her jaw, her chin and all around, but not touching her lips.

Even though she was lying down, Kate felt weak in the knees. Drew took his time, drawing out each movement, each skillful touch, until she was moaning, torn between wanting him to hurry, and to keep doing exactly what he was doing.

He peeled off her wool plaid jacket. Next came her outer oversize blue cotton shirt. Beneath it, she wore a sleeveless undershirt of white, more on the order of a camisole. Ever so slowly, he unbuckled the belt of her jeans and pulled it free. It joined the pile of clothes on the floor.

Drew skimmed his hands over her upper body, soothing every available inch of skin. Her flesh was like satin, smooth and unbelievably warm. He kissed her collarbone, the curve of her elbow, the joint of her wrist.

"Give me a chance," she whispered.

Drew pulled back slightly, adjusting his position, allowing her access to him. "Be my guest."

Kate scrambled up on the bed, watching him watch her, reaching out her hand and then abruptly pulling it back.

"Wait a minute."

He wondered where Kate was going as she scurried off the bed. It was to the window, where she pulled back the curtains, allowing the afternoon sun to spill in. It caught in the foliage outside, gilding the leaves and her hair.

Kate walked back, realizing that she was completely comfortable with him being there.

Drew loomed on the bed. He was big. Powerful. He wore a cream sweater over a pair of well-fitting jeans.

Her gaze dropped.

"I'd say that it's obvious just how much I want you," he said.

She wet her lips. "Looks that way."

Kicking off her shoes, Kate walked back to the bed. She put one knee upon it, then followed with the other so that she rested on them as she sat before him. She slid her hands over the surface of the sweater, gliding them up, around, caressing the entire way.

"Irish?"

"County Cork."

"Hand-knit," she continued, slipping her hands under it, burrowing until she was rewarded with the heated flesh beneath. She stroked her fingertips over his flat stomach, across the tight muscles of his chest, through the dark dusting of hair. It was familiar territory. She could have mapped it out blindfolded.

Drew swallowed, leaning his palms upon the bed, forcing himself to maintain a passive role at that point, letting Kate have her turn at bat. Her touch was deft, sure and so soft. Like the flutter of butterfly wings against his sensitive skin. She circled his masculine nipples, making him catch his breath. One thumb brushed back and forth.

A jolt of intense pleasure followed that action, searing through his body.

Kate raised her head, her eyes bonding with Drew's. Seconds ticked by until he smiled. It was warm, generous, loving.

Kate proceeded then, lifting the well-crafted item up and over his chest. It melded on the floor with her own clothes. Here was the body she'd fantasized over. The body she'd dreamed of. The body she'd written about. All hers now. To love and cherish. To worship and adore.

Kate did just that.

Bending, her lips covered his skin with soft kisses, working her way up and around, over and back.

"I've yearned to do this for so long," she whispered.

"My God, why didn't you say so?"

"Because I thought you wanted to play it safe."

"Safe?" he muttered, drawing her closer. "We haven't played it safe since we met, Kate," he acknowledged. "Safe for both of us would have been to ignore what we felt, pretend that it was just one of those things and gone on with our lives as they were."

"You said that you thought we should get to know each other."

Chagrined, Drew admitted, "I did, didn't I?"

"Damn straight, Tex."

"But it worked, didn't it?"

"What?"

"You see how we are together?" he asked, his hands slipping around to unhook her bra. "Combustible." He pulled the garment apart, then down her arms. "Like a prairie fire gone wild." He pulled Kate close, so that her breasts were touching his chest. "The longer you fan the flames, the brighter the blaze."

"Then, this should be one for the record books," she declared.

"Let's put it to the test."

With a smile that rivaled the best of any big-name Hollywood actress, Kate said, "I thought you'd never ask."

Drew gathered her into his embrace, tumbling them backward onto the comforter, their lips meeting in a kiss that seemed to go on forever. The rest of their clothes were shed as quickly as possible.

Protection achieved, responsibility taken, Drew gazed down at the woman he loved. "You have to believe me, Kate. Never in my life had I felt for any woman what I feel for you. It's not just some line I'm handing you."

"I do believe you, Drew," she responded. Her hand reached up to touch his face, her own feelings shining through, from her blue eyes to her glowing, readable face.

"Then, show me the way home."

And she did.

Kate lay curled up against Drew's broad back, her cheek resting against his skin, one arm around his waist.

Life was good.

No, it was better than good. It was great!

Her bedroom was in darkness, the sun having set a while ago. Kate felt well loved. Muscles slightly sore, lips a trifle swollen from the numerous kisses they had shared. Above all, she felt content. At peace. Or almost.

Being with Drew was like discovering the power of fire. It could warm and cleanse, or burn and destroy. She'd held her hand close to the flames and come away unscathed. Healed.

She realized what her friends and family had repeatedly told her—that she'd shut herself off from taking a chance, from truly living since Jack's death. She'd loved so much and so deeply that she couldn't bear that hurt again if she loved another man and he was snatched from her.

Life didn't always come with promises or pledges. Sometimes you had to have faith. You had to give it another try. Pick up the emotional pieces and carry on as best you could.

And, if you got lucky, you got another shot at the brass ring.

To live life to the fullest was to be vulnerable to hurt, to disappointments, she realized. The secret was to go on because there was a more-than-good chance that love and happiness were also part of the new mix. That's what made life exciting—one didn't know what was in store around the next corner.

Or in the next book tour, she thought with a grin.

She hadn't been looking for a lover—but had found one.

She hadn't been looking for love—but had found it.

Love like this, that most precious of commodities, was worth any risk, any chance. Wasn't that always at the heart of all her stories? Was she any less than one of the strong women she wrote about? Women who bucked odds and circumstances to have the life they wanted, have the relationship they needed.

Not hardly!

She'd tell him later. After dinner.

That made Kate think about the groceries tumbled around the kitchen. She stifled a giggle. What a mess they'd left.

Suddenly Kate remembered the dogs. She'd completely forgotten about Maverick and Iceman as soon as she'd entered the house and gone into Drew's arms.

Easing herself from his body, Kate raised the comforter and sneaked out of the bed. Rummaging through her dresser, she pulled out a nightgown and robe and hastily donned them. She glanced at the sleeping man in her bed and then crept reluctantly out the door.

The dogs were sitting patiently outside the kitchen door when she opened it, looking at her as if to ask what the hell had kept her.

"Sorry, guys. I guess I got a little forgetful."

Kate fixed them a hasty meal, filled their water bowls and built up the fire in the kitchen, the blaze warming the room. She tidied the mess they'd left earlier in their haste to be together, smiling at the stuff littered across the table and the floor. It had certainly been worth the trouble she was now taking.

Everything straightened, food put away, dogs fed, Kate lingered in the room only as long as it took her to find two glasses and haul out the chilled wine from her refrigerator, a white zinfandel.

Entering her bedroom, she saw that Drew was awake.

"Hi."

"Hi, yourself, sweetheart." He tossed back the comforter, making room for her to rejoin him.

Kate's eyes narrowed in appreciation of his glorious naked body. She placed the glasses and opened the bottle of wine on the night table and removed the robe and nightgown quickly.

Seconds later she was where she wanted most in the world to be, in her Lone Star lover's arms.

Chapter Fourteen

"This wasn't quite what I had in mind for our dinner," Kate said by way of apology for the hastily thrown together meal of scrambled eggs and toast. "I wanted to make something very special."

Drew took her hand in his, raised it to his lips and kissed it tenderly, thinking about the kind of ring he wanted to eventually put on her finger. *His* ring. A symbol of the commitment he wanted to make with her. "This is, sweetheart. You and I are here, together, sharing it. That's about as special as it gets, darlin'."

Kate glowed at his softly spoken praise and at the warm feel of his lips on her skin. For her, it was Drew who made every moment special. With him, she was relaxed and happy. Hours spent in his arms, hours spent discovering all over again the magic of San Antonio, had made her so. That, along with finally coming to a decision about where she was going with her life, and with whom.

He sat opposite her, drinking the oversize cup of dark roast coffee she'd made minutes earlier. It was all Kate could do as she ate her eggs not to drool over the image he presented. Big and male. Drew had left his sweater upstairs in her bedroom. All he wore now were his jeans. Her eyes caressed the wide width of his shoulders, brushed over the swirl of sable hair on his chest, lingered on the gleaming gold of the antique cross he wore around his neck. On some men, that particular piece of jewelry would look like an affectation; on Drew, it looked like a slice of living history, a connection to the past.

He released her hand. "What are you thinking?" he asked, intrigued by the sensual heat in her eyes.

Bluntly, Kate replied, "That I love looking at your body."

Drew's fork was suspended halfway to his mouth. He set it back down on the plate untouched. "Say what?"

"You heard me. Shocked you, didn't I?" She laughed softly. "Why, Mr. Buchanan, I do think you're blushing."

"Get real," Drew snorted, picking his fork up and eating the eggs, doing his best to ignore her audacious remark.

"Oh, but I am," Kate shot back, enjoying this verbal banter.

"I'm hardly the type," he retorted, one thick dark brow lifted in a skeptical arc.

"Relax," she said. "I'm only teasing, though," she added, giving him another assessing glance, "I do admit to admiring your magnificent physique."

"Guess that's fine by me," he retorted, "as I can

return the compliment.'' His voice was low and bedroom soft. ''I do like looking at yours, too, sweetheart. With or without the benefit of clothes.''

''Right now,'' she countered, one hand sketching the air as she talked, ''I'm imagining you dressed in a powdered wig and satin, wearing a black mask, dancing the minuet at a fancy dress ball in the governor's mansion in Williamsburg.''

''What?''

Kate smiled. ''I'll let you in on a little secret,'' she confessed. ''The hero in my American Revolution book is physically modeled after you.''

''I'm flattered.''

''Are you?'' she asked. ''Really?''

''Of course,'' he insisted. ''How many men can boast of that?'' Drew buttered another slice of bread from the wicker basket filled with several varieties—wheat, rye and white. ''Unless,'' he observed, ''they're a movie icon or a rock star. I'm sure Brad Pitt and Jon Bon Jovi have fueled many a romance writer's fantasies. I'm neither.''

''Who cares about them?'' she asked. ''You're who *I* want.''

With a slightly rakish look, Drew answered, ''I know.''

Kate placed one hand over the other, resting her chin on them. ''Damn, but you're modest, sweetie.''

''Just tellin' the truth, ma'am,'' he stated, a twinkle in his dark brown eyes. ''We Texans don't brag, we merely state fact.''

''Is that so?'' she inquired with a hint of laughter in her voice.

''Yep.''

"Why do I get the feeling that my chain is being yanked, big time?"

Drew looked at her over the rim of his cup, shrugging those shoulders she loved so much. "Beats me."

"Well, cowboy," she acknowledged, "you're the man of my dreams." Kate bit into a piece of crisp rye toast. "At least," she added with a wicked lift of her brows, "for right now you are." She helped herself to a refill of coffee, adding a splash of cream. "What about you?"

"What about me?"

"Did you ever have a dream woman?"

"No."

Surprise registered on Kate's face at his answer. "You didn't?"

"I can't say that you're the woman of my dreams, Kate—" Drew saw the flash of hurt that clouded her blue eyes at his remark and hastened to explain "—because I didn't really have a notion of a dream until I met you."

She reached over the tabletop and laid her hand on his, squeezing it gently. "What a lovely thing to say."

"It's true, Kate," Drew confessed. "I like women. All kinds, types, what-have-you. There was never one specific *ideal*. Why narrow my opportunities? That's the way I used to think.

"Then," he said, laying his left hand atop hers, "a certain blond writer entered my life. Turned it all upside down, inside out. When you left, I thought that would be the end of it. Memories? Sure. Regrets? Yes. Maybe that it hadn't lasted longer than a few days.

"But you continued to linger in my head. Suddenly, I was measuring other women up to you, and they were falling way short of the mark you'd unknowingly set.

No one had your sweet smile. No one had your earthy laugh or quirky sense of humor. No one had eyes the same shade of blue as yours. No one walked into a room in quite the way you did. And no one made me want as deeply as you had.

"It was useless. They all came up short—through no fault of their own. They couldn't help it. They just weren't you.

"That's when I knew that you'd become my dream, Kate. The one woman I needed to have, the one woman I could really love. You'd spoiled me for any other woman."

Tears wet Kate's eyes. One single fat drop ran down her cheek until she brushed it aside. Drew had so eloquently explained his feelings to her. She owed Drew as much honesty. But where to start? How?

"I don't know what to say."

"I'm not in a hurry, Kate. I told you when I came here that I had time. That hasn't changed."

"I think some part of me loved you on sight. And," she continued, lowering her head for a moment before she lifted it, "another part of me hated you."

Drew inhaled slowly at this revelation. "Why?"

"Because you made me realize that I wasn't as well protected from the desires of the flesh as I thought I was. I'm not talking about finding someone nice-looking, or merely attractive. Thinking that they're hot, or whatever. God knows we all do that as a basic human response." Kate paused, sipping at her coffee, gathering strength to continue. "I'm talking about being so intensely drawn to a person that you can feel it all the way to the deepest reaches of your soul."

She looked down at her half-full cup, staring into it. "You scared me, Drew."

His response was immediate. "I did?"

"My life was fine until that day," she stated, glancing over at him from across the table. "I thought I had everything that I needed. I'd reached a comfortable state of numbness after Jack's death. No man was going to get that close to me again, close enough to make me care. Close enough to make me hurt.

"And then you walked up to that table at the restaurant, as calm as you please, looking like a damned god. Flashing that killer grin, aiming, unknowingly I'm sure, straight for my heart."

Kate abruptly withdrew her hand from his and stood up, clearing the table of their empty plates, stacking them in the sink.

Drew watched as she moved about, busy with mundane matters. She needed a small break, some time to collect her thoughts, he realized. Much as he wanted to make her keep talking, he didn't want to force her. Instead, he focused his attention on the length of long leg that the oversize royal blue sleep-shirt exposed. She'd donned it for comfort instead of the nightgown she'd had on earlier, along with matching flat terry slippers.

"Want some dessert?" she asked as if they hadn't been in the throes of a pointed discussion.

The only dessert Drew wanted right now was Kate, but that could wait. Had to wait until she was ready. "Sure."

Kate dug out a pint of low-fat ice cream from her freezer, one of several that were in there. Grabbing two spoons from the drawer, she placed the ice cream squarely in the middle of the table. "Do you mind sharing?"

"Not in the least, sweetheart," he answered, digging

in. That's what this was all about, his wanting to share with her, everything that mattered to him.

Instead of eating the hearty spoonful that he'd scooped out for himself, Drew held it out toward her lips.

Kate responded with a smile, hastily licking the spoon clean. Reciprocating, she dipped her own spoon into the thick swirl of smooth caramel and chocolate.

As he helped himself to the treat she was offering, Kate said, "You frightened me for another reason Drew—the work you did. Emma told me about Bosnia. That you were wounded there while reporting a story. You like to mix it up in your work, add an element of danger."

He shrugged. "I don't know that I go looking for it."

"Maybe not, but you aren't apt to turn down the work if it includes a risk." Kate observed the dark shadow of beard that hugged his square jaw, the well-defined lips that a short time ago had released a pent-up fervor within her, the thick, long sable brown lashes that framed his eyes. Putting down her spoon, she elevated one hand, her fingertips lightly tracing the outline of his mouth before she pulled them back. "Jack was like that."

"Being a cop entails risk. I'm sure that you knew that when you married him."

"Of course I did," she replied. "But I was in love, and was willing to take the chance that he'd be one of the lucky ones." Kate paused for a moment. "Unfortunately, he wasn't. And I was left to pick up the pieces as best I could.

"At first, I was angry—why did it have to be Jack? He wasn't even supposed to work that day. He went in to help a friend, and on the way in, he responded to a domestic dispute call. A man was holding his wife and son hostage, threatening to kill them. Neighbors had called 911, asking for help. They suspected that the man was on drugs." Her voice quavered slightly with the pain of the memories. "He was."

Drew could see the obvious distress that Kate was in discussing this. "You don't have to tell me now."

"Oh, but I do," she insisted. "I want to be honest with you, Drew. I have to be if we're to have any kind of future."

"Then, perhaps I'd better explain a few things to you, sweetheart."

Kate reached out her hand again and put two fingers to his lips. "Please. Let me do this now."

He nodded his head, backing off, accepting that Kate had to finish what she had started. "Okay."

"Thanks." She dipped her spoon into the pint, savoring the taste, momentarily focusing on something pleasant. "The man was high on drugs. He had a gun, alternately promising to use it on his wife or child. Jack started to talk to him, trying to get him to see reason, or at least the practicality of his situation. Neighbors who witnessed the incident said that they thought Jack was making sense to the man, that he was finally going to give in and let his family go."

Kate stopped, a faraway look in her eyes, as if she were seeing into the past, reliving the day she'd lost her husband.

"Jack got him to eventually let the little boy go. He was just five. Scared out of his mind. He couldn't stop crying. The boy wanted his mama, and Jack asked the man to send out the mother to take care of her son. That seemed to set the man off again. He started to verbally abuse his wife, accusing her of being with other men, of being unfaithful to him with anyone and everyone. Jack tried again to get the man to let her go. By now, other cops had arrived, along with news vans. It had become a circus."

Tears began to fall unchecked down Kate's cheeks as she recounted the events. Her voice was choked with emotion.

Drew wanted to spare her the remembered pain, but he knew that was a futile wish. Just the thought that she'd been hurt so badly angered him. He wanted to amend time, give her back her life as it had been at that point. Anything to spare Kate the agony she'd gone through. Even if it meant she was with another man. But he couldn't change what had happened. So, he listened.

"It was then that everyone thought the man was going to acquiesce. He opened the door, and when Jack approached, the man suddenly went crazy. I was told that the man and his wife were about the same height, so the SWAT snipers couldn't get a clear shot. Not until it was too late. The man started yelling that his wife was no good. He fired and killed Jack instantly."

Drew leaped out of his seat and pulled Kate into his arms, letting her cry out her renewed grief. He rocked her back and forth, his hands comforting on her back, murmuring sweet sounds in her ear. "I'm so sorry, baby," he crooned, holding on to her as she wept.

The dogs reacted to seeing and hearing Kate cry. They both got up and padded over to where Drew now sat, Kate curled into his lap. They stood there, one on either side, vigilant.

Drew handed her a napkin so that she could dry her eyes. "I wish I'd been there for you, Kate."

She relaxed for a second, swallowing the lump that rose in her throat. "You're here now, Drew. That's what matters to me." Kate reached for his cup, drinking the lukewarm coffee that was left. "I found out about it on the news."

"What?" he demanded softly.

"Yeah, great way to learn about one's husband, wasn't it?" she asked with a trace of bitterness. "I came downstairs and turned on the TV while making coffee. I'd overslept that morning because I'd been working on a deadline and had been up till early morning working on the book. There was a note from Jack in the kitchen, on the coffeepot where he knew I'd head first thing, telling me that he'd gone into work, covering for a friend of his whose wife had gone into labor early.

"I'd just sat down with my morning coffee, channel surfing, when I heard the report breaking into the regular programming about a police officer down.

"All of a sudden I got a very cold feeling. Some part of me wanted to turn off the set. That if I could shut off the TV, then it wouldn't be happening. Stupid, wasn't it?"

"No," Drew answered, his own eyes misted with moisture. "It was human, darlin'."

"I sat there, frozen, unable to do anything but watch. They didn't identify the officer, but I caught a glimpse of the gurney that was being loaded into the ambulance. I saw a hand sticking out beneath the sheet. It was wearing a ring, a gold *cladagh* ring. Just like the one I gave Jack on our honeymoon in Ireland."

Drew's heart was aching for her, seeing the picture of her in his mind's eye. Alone, frightened, finding out about her husband's death from the TV.

"All I could think about then was that I hadn't said goodbye to him that morning. I always made a point of saying goodbye to Jack whenever he went on duty. In his note, he told me that he hadn't wanted to wake me because he knew I'd worked so very late the night before. He wanted me to get my sleep. He'd see me later that day. And he added that he loved me.'' Kate adjusted her position so that she was looking directly into Drew's eyes. ''I never got a chance to tell him that I loved him that last time. The one day I should have said it. The one day it would have mattered.''

''It mattered, sweetheart, every time you said it,'' he assured her. ''It wasn't your fault.''

''But don't you see,'' she argued, ''I should have been there for him.''

''Knowing you as I do,'' Drew said, ''you were, Kate. Jack Terrelli probably considered himself the luckiest man alive because *you* loved him. Whether or not you said it that morning, he knew how you felt. How could he not? You don't have a thing to feel guilty about.''

''You're the only person whom I've told about this, Drew. I couldn't tell anyone else. It was too painful. And I was too ashamed, feeling as if I'd failed him that day.''

''You didn't. You couldn't.'' He stroked her hair, kissing it. ''Let it go, Kate. I don't think your Jack would have wanted you to cling to the pain forever.''

''I don't know if I ever can.''

''Yes, you do,'' he stated emphatically. ''You can do anything, darlin'. You're one of the country's bestselling writers. Getting to that spot isn't easy.''

''You know, that's what kept me going right after it happened. My work. I buried myself in it, seeking solace in a world where I could control events. Good people triumphed, evil got its just rewards.''

''Unlike the real world we live in,'' he commented.

Kate nodded her head in agreement. ''So I do know how much your work means to you, Drew. I've thought about it since we first met.''

"I can't deny that it's what gives—or should I say *gave*—me the most pleasure," he stated. "Writing is what I do best."

"I realize that," she said, laying her head on his broad chest, listening to the tempo of his heartbeat, steady under her ear. Sure and strong. Just like Drew. A man to cross bridges with. A man to rebuild dreams with. A man to share all the burdens and all the joys of life with.

"What you do," she said, "is who you are. Like me. Your work is important."

"But," he countered, "it isn't the only thing in my life, Kate. Not any longer. That changed the day I met you."

She loved hearing that. Having realized that if she loved the man, she had to accept all there was about him, especially that which defined him. His work. Every aspect of it, whether or not she liked all of it or what it entailed. Drew respected who and what she was. If she cared as much for him, she could do no less.

"Remember I said that what you did scared me? That's because," she explained, "I was afraid that I'd fallen into another relationship that would only end in pain. You liked what you did. You were good at it. A danger junkie at times. What mattered to you was the story. When we were together that weekend, that's all I thought that we'd have. There didn't seem to be any future in it. I wasn't looking for a long-term thing, and neither, I suspect, were you."

"No, I wasn't," he answered truthfully.

"So, when I realized that I was falling in love with you, I didn't see it going anywhere. I couldn't get past my fear of being with a man who could be put in harm's way at any time. I couldn't invest any more of myself with someone who might leave me alone, again. I'd been through that once. The vow I'd made to myself was never, ever, again.''

"What changed your mind?"

"You," she emphasized, "among other things."

Drew lifted her chin and stared down into her eyes. "When did you decide this?"

"Earlier today."

"Thank God. I didn't know how much longer I could have held out, sweetheart."

"Held out?"

"Exactly. I wanted to be with, *really* with you, but I was afraid that you'd think that's all I wanted, a pickup of our affair. If I went slow, then I figured you'd see that I wasn't in this just for the sex. It never occurred to me that you had a problem with my work."

"Because it was something that I had to work on, Drew. It's my fear. Not yours."

"But don't you see," he offered, "that you didn't feel as though you could trust me?"

Kate hastened to reassure him. "No. I do trust you, or we wouldn't be here. It's my problem."

"If it affects you and me, then it's *our* problem," he said. "And I can tell you that you don't have to worry about it any longer."

Kate misconstrued his words, interrupting him. "Easier said than done, but I'm going to try my damnedest to make it happen."

"Listen," he tried to interject.

"No, let me finish," she said. "You love your work and I can't try and take that from you. If someone asked me to give up who and what I was for them, I couldn't. What's more, I wouldn't. I don't have the right to ask you to rearrange your life for me. That's not love, Drew."

Kate cupped his face. "And I do love you. More than I thought I ever could again. More than my fears. What frightens me now is thinking about a life without you. A life devoid of the love that we can share. To have that, I'm willing to take chances." She stared deeply into his eyes. "After all, I can't wrap you up in a nice, safe protective shell and expect that you'll thank me for that. You wouldn't be the man I fell in love with if you did. Accidents of fate happen, things that we can't control. I can't change that, much as I may want to. Nor, I realized, can I stop living, or loving. I've been given a very special gift. A second chance."

"I can't promise that nothing will ever happen to me," Drew said, "because I don't know the future. But," he stated, framing her face, too, lightly kissing her mouth, "I think that I can alleviate some of your misgivings about my career."

"What are you talking about?"

Drew stroked one hand through her hair. "When I was single, with no one to answer to except myself, I did as I pleased. Roots weren't a priority, especially in terms of relationships. You changed that. After that weekend, things altered. Roots began to seem like something that I *could* live with. Wanted to experience. In thinking about that, I discovered I needed to try something different. Accept a new challenge to go with my new maturity, for want of a better word.

"I contacted a literary agent and talked to her about representing me in a nonfiction proposal that I had in mind, a sort of biography. She liked the idea and took it on. So, if it sells, then I plan on taking a sabbatical from the magazine and spending my time writing this book. If I like how it comes out, then I may have a new career. One that will give us more time together. Think you could handle that, sweetheart?''

Kate's heart swelled with joy. "Oh, I think I could get used to the idea.''

"I hope so, since we'll be sharing that same agent.''

"What?''

"I got her name from a novel you dedicated to her. I asked her to keep it between us in case the idea fell through.''

"Why did you pick her?''

"To feel closer to you,'' he confessed.

Kate threw her arms about his neck and hugged him. "How did I get so lucky?''

"You came to Texas, sweetheart.''

"Is that it?'' she asked.

"Damn straight,'' he drawled.

"Good thing I did, then,'' she conceded. "Life without you, Mr. Buchanan, would have been empty and dull indeed. Like a dash of chili pepper, you add spice.''

"Is it spice you're looking for, Ms. Reeves?'' Drew stood up and placed Kate's posterior on the table.

She tilted her head up, wondering what he was up to.

A devilish grin kicked up his mouth. "Let's see about that.'' He called to the dogs, escorting them out of the kitchen and into another adjoining room, shutting the door upon his return.

"Why'd you take Iceman and Maverick into the laundry room?''

"For privacy.''

Kate leaned back, legs dangling over the edge of the wooden table, palms flat. "You have something in mind?''

"Most definitely, sweetheart.''

Kate wet her lips. "Am I going to like it?''

Drew approached her, moving closer, reaching out his hands and gently lifting her face up for his kiss. "You're gonna love it."

"You're sure?" she demanded in a softly challenging tone, her heartbeats increasing in anticipation of the action to follow.

"Word of a Texan, sweetheart."

"That's good enough for me, cowboy."

He leaned over her, one arm scattering the half-eaten pint of ice cream and spoons to the floor. The basket of bread followed, along with napkins and the salt and pepper shakers.

"Right here?" she asked, hands already reaching to draw him close.

"Right now," he whispered huskily, sealing the promise with a kiss that healed the past and forged the future.

Kate smiled wickedly as she checked her E-mail a few hours later. She didn't think she would see her kitchen table in quite the same light again. They'd followed that exciting adventure up with a quick shower. At least, it had started off as quick, she recalled.

Drew had gotten a call, so she left him alone to take it, deciding to walk down the hall and into her office. She read her messages, scanned the pages and stopped at the last entry. It had been sent only minutes before. From her mystery man.

"Come live with me and be my love."

She sat there, wondering how and what to answer.

"What's wrong?" Drew asked, strolling into her office, resting on a corner of her big desk as she stared at the computer screen.

Kate's expression was one filled with warmth as she

tilted her head sideways and regarded her lover. "Another message from Wizard."

"You don't say."

Kate's jaw dropped when Drew repeated the words verbatim that the man had sent.

"How did you know?" she demanded, stunned. "I just received it."

"Because I just sent it," he answered.

"*You* sent it?"

Drew nodded. "That's right, sweetheart. I have a laptop, too. Remember?"

"It's been you all along?"

He got up and came over to her, hunkering down. "I wanted to reach you in a special way. To show you that you're always on my mind, even if you weren't there with me. You gotta admit, Kate, I got you hooked, didn't I?"

Kate laughed. "I should be mad, I suppose, but I'm more flattered. Why Wizard, though?"

"It was the male equivalent of enchantress, the English translation for Encantadora, the Spanish name for our ranch. An in-joke, if you will. I didn't want you to figure it out too easily."

Kate turned around and went back to her keyboard, quickly typing in a response.

"What's that?"

"Your answer."

Drew stood up and looked over her shoulder, reading the response. It was the answer he'd been searching for; the only answer he'd desired, or needed.

"*Yes!!!*"

Epilogue

He stood there, the embodiment of her dreams, the dreams she'd thought forever lost to her when a drunken gunslinger had robbed her of her husband, and the town of its sheriff. Pride stamped his face; courage radiated from every lean line of muscle; strength of will showed in his eyes. The war, she knew, had taken its toll on him, as it had everyone else in Santa Rosa.
He wanted a fresh start, a new beginning.
So did she.

"I just can't believe that your parents are doing all this," Kate said, glancing up from the keyboard of her laptop when Drew walked into the bedroom of the guest house in San Antonio, where, for memories' sake, they'd decided to stay when they flew into town yesterday. She

was hard at work on her next novel, set in Texas duri.
the aftermath of the Civil War, and Drew was busy with
his own project, researching his family history for the
book he was writing.

It was mid-May and the temperature was already in
the high eighties. Sultry, with the promise of even more
steam later in the day. A change from the weather back
home in Pennsylvania, where it was still moderately
warm.

Kate sat at the small table in comfortable terry shorts
and a T-shirt, her thick, curly hair held back with two
combs. A large glass of iced tea, half drunk, was at her
hand.

"Believe it, sweetheart," Drew stated, bending down
to give his fiancée a quick, hard kiss, and then draining
her glass. "It's not every day that one of their sons gets
married, and here in Texas, we do it up right."

"I think you mean *big*, don't you?" Kate teased, secretly thrilled with the grand engagement party that Santina and Noah Buchanan were throwing later that night
at the family ranch in the Hill Country. She was over-
joyed at being welcomed into this close-knit family,
looking forward to the day when she would marry Drew
Buchanan, the man who'd reaffirmed her belief in love
and happiness, in the power of second chances.

"Remember, I've got lots of relatives hereabouts, not
to mention friends, all of whom are dying to meet you."

Kate stood up, a wide smile on her mouth as she
melted into her lover's arms. "You mean, it's gonna be
quite a bit larger than the one Mariah threw for us in
Philly?" Kate stood on tiptoe and kissed his freshly
shaven cheek.

"I kinda think so, darlin'," Drew murmured slyly, his
arms holding her close to his heart, where she belonged.

What a different track his life had taken in just over a year—and all because of this woman. He, who'd formerly shunned commitment, was now going to take the ultimate step, marriage. He, who'd liked to travel, to get up and go, with no one to answer to save himself, had settled down to a wonderful life of domestic harmony with Kate, relocating to her area of the country, adapting to her situation.

Of course, it wasn't always smooth sailing; they were two passionate, strongly opinionated people, and writers to boot, each with their own lives. But because they loved each other, they were willing to work on the relationship. They'd both fought too hard to have this love to ever give up on it.

One by one, Drew thought, the Buchanan brothers were stepping up to the matrimonial altar, hitching their lives to the women they loved—and who loved them.

Now the only one left was Clay, the oldest.

"We'd better be leaving soon if we want to get to the ranch in plenty of time," Kate said, stepping back reluctantly.

Drew reached for her. "They'll wait for us."

Kate rolled her eyes, arms akimbo.

Drew recognized the determined look on Kate's face. "We won't be late, I promise. I have a little something to give you that I want to be between us." He pulled out a tiny box from the back pocket of his jeans and handed it to her.

"What's this?" she asked, looking at the plain white box.

"Open it up and see," he instructed, a deep grin on his face.

Kate did. Surprise registered on her face when she saw

he contents and read the tiny note folded inside. "Is this a joke?"

"No."

Kate lifted her head, staring into his eyes. "How did you arrange it?"

"Can't reveal my sources, sweetheart," he stated dramatically. "Let's just say that it was all worth it to see the look on your face right now."

She picked up the tiny pair of gold wings from inside the box. "I can't believe it."

"Believe it," he declared.

"A ride with the Blue Angels in an honest-to-God supersonic jet." Kate glanced back down at the lapel pin she held in her hand, along with the note, and then whooped, "Yes!" tossing the tiny box into the air. She jumped into Drew's arms, her legs riding high on his waist.

Drew, his hands cupping her bottom, whirled her around. "I thought that would bring a smile to your face, sweetheart."

"You, my loving Texas man," she said, her blue eyes filled with love, "you bring a smile to my face. Each and every day." Kate, one arm around Drew's back, holding on, the other clutching the pin and the slightly crumpled paper in her left hand, the hand that wore the ruby-and-platinum ring he'd put there several weeks ago.

They'd been living together, one day at a time; each knowing the goal they wanted to achieve, the next step, would happen when the moment was right.

It had been the day the galley pages for her new hardcover had arrived and she'd shown the dedication page to Drew.

This book is for the man who taught me to value each and every new day; who showed me that love, like a phoenix, can rise and be reborn; who gave me hope and the greatest gift of all—his heart.

This book, along with all my love, is for you, Drew.

Kate let the scrap of paper and the pin fall to the floor as she wound her arms around his neck, leaning closer. Her lips tasted his skin; her tongue stroked a path along his strong jaw to his ear. "I've changed my mind."

"About what?" Drew demanded, turning slowly and heading for the bed.

"Rushing to the party," she whispered. "You're right. They can wait. This is important."

Tumbling them both to the comfort of the plump mattress, Drew responded huskily, "Damn straight, sweetheart."

*   *   *   *   *

Bestselling author

JOAN JOHNSTON

continues her wildly popular miniseries with an
all-new, longer-length novel

The Virgin Groom

HAWK'S WAY

One minute, Mac Macready was a living legend in
Texas—every kid's idol, every man's envy, every
woman's fantasy. The next, his fiancée dumped him,
his career was hanging in the balance and his future
was looking mighty uncertain. Then there was the
matter of his scandalous secret, which didn't stand a
chance of staying a secret. So would he succumb to
Jewel Whitelaw's shocking proposal—or take cold
showers for the rest of the long, hot summer…?

Available August 1997
wherever Silhouette books are sold.

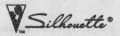

Look us up on-line at: http://www.romance.net

HAWK

New York Times **bestselling author**

SANDRA BROWN

brings a love story that will take you...

ABOVE AND BEYOND

(previously published under the pseudonym Erin St. Claire)

Letters of love—to another man—brought them together. A powerful secret may tear them apart.

Trevor Rule fell in love with Kyla before he met her, just by reading the letters she'd written to her husband—Trevor's best friend. Now he had to convince Kyla that they both had the right to be happy and move past the tragedy of Trevor's death....

Available in September 1997
at your favorite retail outlet.

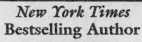

Silhouette

SPECIAL EDITION™

WELCOME TO SILVER CREEK COUNTY

A place full of small-town Texas charm, where
everybody knows your name and falling
in love is all in a day's work!

Popular author **SHARON DE VITA** has
spun several delightful stories full of matchmaking
kids, lonely lawmen, single parents and humorous
townsfolk! Watch for the third book,
ALL IT TAKES IS FAMILY (Special Edition
#1126, 9/97). And if you missed the first two books,
THE LONE RANGER (Special Edition #1078, 1/97)
and **THE LADY AND THE SHERIFF** (Special Edition
#1103, 5/97), be sure to pick up your copies today!

Come on down to Silver Creek and make
a few friends—you'll be glad you did!